SMALL GAME

SMALL GAME

A NOVEL

BLAIR BRAVERMAN

ecco

An Imprint of HarperCollinsPublishers

SMALL GAME. Copyright © 2022 by Blair Braverman. All rights reserved. Printed in the United States of America. No part of this book may be used or reproduced in any manner whatsoever without written permission except in the case of brief quotations embodied in critical articles and reviews. For information, address HarperCollins Publishers, 195 Broadway, New York, NY 10007.

HarperCollins books may be purchased for educational, business, or sales promotional use. For information, please email the Special Markets Department at SPsales@harpercollins.com.

Ecco® and HarperCollins® are trademarks of HarperCollins Publishers.

FIRST EDITION

Designed by Angela Boutin

Title Page Illustration © PikePicture/stock.adobe.com

Library of Congress Cataloging-in-Publication Data has been applied for.

ISBN 978-0-06-306617-5

22 23 24 25 26 LSC 10 9 8 7 6 5 4 3 2 1

for Q
and Flame
my survival partners

SMALL GAME

1

Ashley wanted to be famous. That's not an insult, it's the truth. She said so herself on the first night, sitting cross-legged by the fire after the cameras left. Back when they were all still new to each other. She said, "I'm here to get famous, aren't you?" Mara had never heard anyone talk about fame that way, like it was something you could earn and spend. But that was Ashley, or how she used to be. Practical, even in the woods.

The funny thing is that it probably would have worked. Ashley was magazine-gorgeous, with this earnest charm, like she saw everyone for who they wanted to be instead of who they were. Someone like that, once the world noticed her, she could write her ticket. She'd smuggled a folding comb in her bra and buried it behind camp, so she could smooth her long hair each morning before the camera crew came back. She said it was her job to look good.

Then there was Kyle. Kyle was an Eagle Scout, which

meant a lot to him, although none of the others even pretended to care. A skinny kid with red hair and perfect posture. He was nineteen, from Indiana, and he had a way of waiting after people spoke, just a beat too long, to see if they were finished talking. It was meant to be polite, but it creeped Mara out. She had always felt most comfortable around people who ignored her.

Bullfrog was a carpenter from Michigan. He barely talked to his teammates those first weeks, though he talked to the cameras. He was a real anarchist type, old-school. The kind who wouldn't call it anarchy, just country living or "fuck the government" or something like that. Mara didn't understand why he'd want to be on a reality show. It took her a long time to make sense of Bullfrog at all.

There was a fifth guy, too. James. Probably out thriving somewhere. You wouldn't think he'd be the most painful for Mara to think about, but that's how it goes. He was the only one who got out in time.

THE SHOW WAS CALLED *CIVILIZATION*. THEIR CLOTHES WERE FAST-FASHION PREHIS-toric, canvas tunics and matching shorts, all dyed a dusty brown. And sandals made of thin leather, so they had to walk delicately, toe first, like girls playing fairies. The idea was that they'd found one another in the wilderness, this group of strangers, and over the course of six weeks would be tasked with building a new kind of community, something pure and sustainable and right. They would forgo all comforts, so that viewers didn't have to. They would be one with the forest. They would find a way to live.

Presumably the process would reveal something about the

dawn of civilization. What society would look like if it were made from scratch, that sort of thing. How it might be different. You could practically hear the pitch meeting.

But really it was just a survival show. That's what they told Mara in the auditions. She said, "Look, I'm not trying to rebuild society. I'm just trying to get out of it." She had plenty to get away from. Her boyfriend, Ethan, for one thing, who was the real survival geek of the two of them. The casting agent said, "Don't worry about the conceit. How are you at building shelters? Have you ever used snares?" Of course she had, and he knew that. So she mumbled along, and she must have fit whatever slot they were looking to fill. Young woman with experience, not beautiful, to balance out Ashley, who was beautiful but inexperienced. They must have done that with the men, too. The Eagle Scout, the math teacher, the old grouch who had a heart of gold—or with the right edits, the right music, they could make it seem like he did. The survivors might as well have introduced themselves by their archetypes.

At the time the show found Mara, she was living in a camper with Ethan pretty deep in the woods. The camper wasn't road-worthy, but they'd built two walls and a roof around it, so it stayed dry even in the soggy Washington winter. They had lived there three years at that point, and the camper felt smaller each season. They were always in each other's way. They did laundry in a pond and smoked too much. It bothered Ethan that Mara had grown up off-grid, whereas he'd come to the lifestyle for the aesthetic, or at least that's what she said when they fought. But he had the dedication of a convert. He was always coming up with new ideas—solar ovens, beehives, a greenhouse made of reclaimed windows from the dump. She wanted a dishwasher.

Four days a week, Ethan and Mara worked at a survival school run by a former blockchain developer named Bjørn. They taught classes sometimes, trapping and fire-building and so on, but the school's biggest business was leaving clients in the woods overnight. There were always people willing to pay for the experience: a steady stream of tech bros, spiritual seekers, and corporate burnouts from Seattle, for whom camping itself would have felt too banal. If they paid good money, their night outside was recognized, celebrated.

In the mornings, Mara gathered clients from their assigned sites and made them scrambled eggs over a campfire, assuring them that they had indeed conquered the wilderness, though a fair number spent the night shivering, and never built or caught anything at all. Then she gave out braided leather bracelets in a fireside ceremony. She could tell people treasured them. Like they'd wear their bracelets to the office on Monday, and touch them throughout the day to remind themselves who they really were.

Civilization's casting team came to the survival school, which was called Primal Instinct, to search for talent. They brought the instructors one by one into a hotel room, sat them on the edge of a bed, and asked for their life stories. Just the highlights: age, family, hobbies, trauma. They must have liked Mara's, because the next day they called her back to the hotel. The room was disheveled by then, and the bedspread less crisp.

"So tell me," said the casting agent from behind a giant lens. He wore a blazer and sipped an energy drink through a straw. "What skills would you bring to this challenge?"

He told her to answer in full sentences, as if she were not responding to a question at all, but simply thinking aloud.

"I would bring many skills to the challenge," said Mara, feeling uncomfortable. "For instance, I'm good at foraging." She was good at a lot of things outdoors, but foraging was the first that came to mind.

"That's good," he said. "That's a start. Can you say it with more conviction?"

Mara sat up straighter, which was hard, because the edge of the bed sloped down. "I'm very good at foraging."

"Do you think you can last six weeks out there?"

"Probably."

"Probably?"

"Anything could happen. I could get struck by lightning. But I think my odds are good."

"What would you say your odds are?"

"Better than most."

"Full sentences. And look, you do you, but if you could sound more confident—"

She was trying.

"I will last six weeks in the challenge," Mara said. Then, when he didn't respond, "I know for a fact that I can last six weeks out there, whatever happens. I've done it before and I'll do it again."

That wasn't strictly accurate. Mara rarely slept outside the camper when she wasn't working; she didn't see the point. But the agent liked it.

"Great," he said. "Perfect. Do you want to add anything about making nature your bitch?"

"I'd rather not," she said.

"Okay," he said, glancing at his notes. "That was promising, Mary. That'll do for now."

She did not expect to hear from him again. But a few

weeks later, the show's producer, Lenny, called and told her she'd made the cut. She had three days to commit or decline.

Bjørn was thrilled. Having an instructor on television would be a boon for Primal Instinct. He could offer special promotions, and host a public viewing party with chaga beer and cricket chips for snacks. He'd charge a premium for Mara's classes. Even rebrand the school around the show, if it came to that. He asked Mara to mention Primal Instinct by name as many times as she could.

When Mara told Ethan the news, he went outside and didn't come back all afternoon. She took a nap on the futon, pleased to have the camper to herself. By evening he was ready to talk.

"I'm just concerned," he said. "I don't want them to take advantage of you. Don't you think it's degrading? Going out there for everyone to see? Living like we do, it's . . . it's sacred. It's not a publicity stunt."

"Then why did you interview for the show?"

"That was an experiment," he said. "I wouldn't say yes if they asked me."

Mara liked that it bothered him, and that he couldn't stop her. She hadn't put much hope in the interview process—she'd assumed that, like most things, it wouldn't work out—but now that she had a choice, it gave her a warm sense in her belly, and even more so because Ethan disapproved. Besides, there was prize money. Anyone who made it six weeks got a hundred grand. She thought she'd leave Ethan if she made it, start over with the cash, and maybe he sensed that.

She called Lenny and told him she wanted in. She was going to be in *Civilization*'s opening cast, part of a brand-new journey. "This will be the hardest thing you ever do," Lenny told her.

"Of course," she said. But she doubted it.

LENNY ASKED MARA TO FILM HERSELF GETTING READY, BUT SINCE THE DETAILS OF the show were meant to be a surprise, she wasn't sure how to prepare. She mostly walked around the property and showed off things she had already done. Ethan made sure she introduced him. "This is our wood-fired hot tub we built," she said, and he added, from outside the frame, "We built it together," like she hadn't just said that. Ethan had a structure behind the camper, a medieval-style roundhouse that he'd worked on sporadically for years. It wasn't finished, but it was still impressive, with stone walls and a pointy roof. She could tell that Ethan wanted her to film it, but she didn't. In her mind she had already won the money, and could afford to distinguish between what was hers and what was his.

Lenny sent an eighty-page contract, which Mara was meant to sign in a dozen places and return. She read some of it, then skipped to the part about the prize. There it was: one hundred thousand dollars. With money like that, she'd have options. She could get her GED. There was a community college nearby with a two-year program in wind turbines, and she'd heard that its graduates did well. Mara didn't care about wind turbines, but she thought she'd be good at the job—working alone, fixing things. She had always been quick to learn.

That was how she felt about survivalism, too. It wasn't that she was naturally talented, though she knew she was better than most people, and was probably the best instructor at Primal Instinct. She just spent a lot of time in the woods, and she wasn't upset about being uncomfortable or working hard. It was easy for her to do one task and then another, and then another, which was the way to get through most things in life. She didn't overthink.

At work, her clients overthought everything. They got cold and some part of them feared they'd be cold forever. They used terms like *starvation mode* after half a day, and they meant it. When their campouts ended, they were either thrilled or morose, with no middle ground. Mara never understood how a client could be disappointed in the morning. After all, they'd set out to stay in the woods overnight, and they'd succeeded. But clearly there was something else that clients wanted, and no way to gauge from the outside if they found it or not.

The happiest clients weren't the ones who gathered food, or even made a nice fire, but the ones who built things. Who shaped nature, even slightly, into a form that served or inspired them. A good shelter could do that: a debris hut on a cold night, with mounds of dry leaves to hold in warmth. Or a lean-to on a rainy afternoon: that damp, solid feeling of drops striking all the world but you.

One time Mara went to retrieve a client and found her in a garden made of stones. It must have been ten feet across, a labyrinth of pebbles, a spiral with waves extending out like the rays of a sun. The woman sat cross-legged in the middle, smiling, though she had no shelter or water or food. But she seemed content in a way Mara had rarely seen. When Mara gave her a bracelet, she kissed it before tying it around her wrist, and then she closed her eyes.

Later Mara brought other instructors to see the stones. Normally they took camps apart after clients left, unweaving branches and burying the remains of fires, but none of them wanted to break the maze. So they left it untouched, and stopped bringing people to that spot. Mara often wondered if the stones were still there.

For a while she told other clients about the labyrinth, hoping they'd try something similar. Mostly they were dismissive. "I'm here to survive, not play with rocks," a guy told her, like she was the one who didn't get it. Like surviving the night was some big achievement, when it was far easier than making something beautiful. The secret to survival, Mara thought, was that it was hard to die. Even if you gave in, gave up, just sat there and waited for it. You could be waiting a long time.

2

On her last shift before leaving for the show, Mara was assigned to supervise three Ultimates with her friend Simone. Ultimate was the most advanced package that Primal Instinct offered, and also the most expensive, though it required from instructors the least amount of work. Clients had to sleep outside for two nights without a tent, and with limited supplies: a tin cup, a knife, fishing line and one hook, matches, and their choice of tarp or wool blanket. Mara thought the blanket was better, though few people picked it. Sometimes they even declined the matches, saying they'd build a primitive fire instead. That was when Mara knew they were in for a rough weekend.

Ultimates cost nine hundred dollars per person. But no one complained about the cost, not like they did with classes and basic overnights, which were much cheaper. They expected to be transformed, and everyone knew that transformation was expensive. Clients were glad to pay. These weren't all people with money, either. Some of them had saved for a year.

Mara liked doing Ultimates, especially with Simone. They hung out in the company van, parked in the shoulder of a dirt road, and three times a day made rounds of the clients' sites to make sure no one was panicking or hurt. If a client wanted help or company, they offered it. But mostly they waved and moved on, or even crept by unnoticed. That week their shift started Saturday morning, after the clients' first night. Mara and Simone left the van an hour after dawn and headed into the woods for rounds. The sky was bright, and columns of sunlight shone through openings in the leaves.

Mara carried a first aid kit, water, and bags of trail mix, though she wouldn't offer supplies unless asked. She also brought a live snake in a cotton bag. If a client seemed too discouraged, Simone would distract them, and Mara would release the snake into their camp.

The snakes they brought weren't venomous. They were gopher snakes, native to the northwest, and came special-ordered from a pet store. Mara hated buying them. The teenagers at checkout were earnest, and had been trained to ask questions. Do you have a heat lamp? they asked. Do you have bedding? And Mara would nod and say yes, yes, this isn't my first snake. I understand that a snake is a lifetime responsibility. I am prepared to give this snake what it needs. It was true that Bjørn had terrariums back at headquarters. But the longest they'd kept a snake was a month, and that was in January, when business was slow.

Instructors weren't supposed to release a snake unless a client really needed a boost. But when they did, the snake made a big difference. Usually one of two things happened.

One, a client killed and ate it, or killed it, took a proud bite, and discarded the rest. Bjørn picked gopher snakes in particular because they were large, easy to pin with a branch, even for those with untrained reflexes.

More often, clients didn't catch the snake, but they came out with a story. When two clients were together, Mara could watch it go down. "Did you see that?" one would ask.

And the other: "Is there a chance it was a rattlesnake?"

"I couldn't tell."

"Me neither."

"Actually, yeah, I think—you saw the rattle, right?" Constructing a truth in real time, lying so they could both believe it. Then they were happy. Probably the snake was, too. It could slither off and eat rats for a decade until someday getting eaten by a hawk.

That weekend, the first Ultimate consisted of a dad and his teenage son, which was a pretty standard combination. They camped by a pond—a decent site, plenty of bluegills, though it shimmered with mosquitos in all but the hottest hours of the day. Mara waved through the trees, and the dad lifted a hand, but there was no urgency to his wave. All good.

The second duo was an older couple, who had asked not to be interrupted. It always made Mara nervous when couples said that, because she had to check on them anyway, and it meant they might be fucking. She found them by a fire in a dense grove, their eyes closed, chanting words she didn't know. The man rested his palms on his wife's wrists. It was too intimate; it made Mara uncomfortable. She was glad to slip away.

The last location was one of her favorites. A waterfall bounced down mossy boulders and landed in a pool full of newts. When the sun was low, the spray cast rainbows. The newts wiggled to the surface and then drifted back down, dozens of them, rising and falling in waves. Newts were poisonous, so you couldn't eat them, but Mara could watch for hours and not get bored.

This was a single Ultimate, a man who'd come alone. But when Mara and Simone reached the waterfall, there was nobody there. Simone found the wool blanket folded neatly by a tree, with a cup and a knife beside it. It wasn't uncommon for clients to go walking, but normally they brought their knives.

"What do you think?" said Simone. "Wait or go?"

"Let's go," said Mara. "I don't mind coming back." If they didn't set eyes on a client, they had to return an hour later. If the client was still missing, they called Bjørn. He always had his phone.

"You sure?"

"Yeah. It's no problem." Mara felt oddly restless. She didn't want to wait.

Back at the van, Simone put her feet on the dash. There were cots in the back, but during the day they liked to sit up front and eat Red Vines. Usually Simone complained about her boyfriend, in the way people complain about someone they really love. He was an aspiring playwright who worked at a drag bar downtown. But today Simone seemed thoughtful.

"Are you nervous?" she asked.

She meant about *Civilization*.

"It'll be fine," said Mara. "It's nothing new."

"Not the nature part. The television part. How many people will watch it? Millions? I'd be freaking out."

"I don't really care either way."

"I don't believe that," said Simone.

"Can we not?"

"Jeez," she said. "Sorry."

Mara felt bad for snapping. She opened the snake bag and found the snake curled tight in the bottom. It was heavy and cool and she put it on Simone's lap. Simone liked snakes.

"We could name it," Mara said.

"What letter are we on?"

"*W*, I think."

"Wes. Walt. Willow."

"I like Wes," said Mara. "It's simple."

"Maybe you have ideas."

"No, I like Wes."

They were both trying to be nice. Mara was glad when an hour passed and she had an excuse to leave.

When she got to the waterfall, the newts were having a party. The water's surface was dimpled with their heads. But there was no sign of the client. Mara braced herself and called Bjørn. He got irritable when they lost people in the woods.

Bjørn was chewing when he answered the phone.

"Oh, him," said Bjørn. He swallowed. "He left first thing this morning. Just walked out. I thought I told you. He wasn't fucked up or anything. He said, I forget, something positive, though. That he realized this wasn't where he needed to be."

Mara could tell that Bjørn knew exactly what the client had said. He kept track of what clients said when they were happy. If they changed their minds, he could remind them.

The next morning, Mara and Simone gathered the remaining duos for a breakfast bonfire and presented them with their bracelets. The couple held hands the whole time. The man kissed his wife's hair, shyly, like he couldn't resist. Like the world was theirs alone. The dad kept asking about the guy who left. Mara said she couldn't share details, but he stayed on it.

"See?" he told his son. "Not everyone can do what we just did. They can't handle it."

After work, Mara dropped Wes off at headquarters, setting him in the nicest terrarium, and bought a sandwich and a milkshake for the drive home. But when she got to the camper, Ethan was grilling pork chops. So she ate again, though she was full. Then she sucked Ethan off on the futon. He touched her hair and kissed her, and she stroked his neck the way he liked, and when they were done she put her head on his chest. The next day she left, hopefully for good.

3

There was a big deal about how Mara couldn't know where she was going. In retrospect she wished she had tried to find out. But what difference would it make? She hoped the show would be set somewhere tropical, or at least exotic, where the novelty of the environment could offset its inevitable miseries. She imagined coconuts with their rich meat, turquoise water to the horizon, and biting sand fleas. A red desert with its venoms and frigid nights. Somewhere far away and nothing like home.

Instead she flew to Green Bay, Wisconsin, on a day's notice, and slept in an airport hotel room that had been reserved in her name. In the morning she found a box outside her door with a tunic and matching shorts, brown underwear and a brown sports bra, and handmade leather sandals. She tugged the clothes into place before the bathroom mirror. They fit, mostly. The shorts were snug. She wondered who had decided that everything had to be brown.

Around noon she got a call to go to the parking lot, where a woman in a velour sweatsuit picked her up with a four-door pickup. The woman eyed Mara's backpack. "That all you got?"

"They said I didn't need anything."

"Put your phone and wallet in there, too. I'll take it."

"I get it back, right?"

"Sure," said the woman. She gave Mara a blindfold to cover her eyes.

That was the last thing she said for a while. She didn't talk as they drove. Then her phone rang, and she answered on the first ring. "Yeah," she said. "Yeah. I have number three. On track." She hung up without saying goodbye.

By the sun's warmth through the window, Mara figured they were driving north. She didn't mind the silence. She went over her plan in her head—not for surviving nature, but for surviving the show. Though she hadn't wanted to admit it, Simone was right. The show was her greater concern.

Mara felt confident she could make it six weeks in the wild, save some injury or television plot device. She trusted reality shows about as much as she trusted anything, which was to say she assumed everyone was in it for themselves, and if she wasn't in charge, or paying, then she was being used. That didn't bother her. In this case, it was almost reassuring. She knew her role; her role was entertainment. She was there for the producer, who was there for money, which meant he was there for the audience. Mara was disposable.

She hoped to use the dynamic to her advantage. She would be unmemorable, and by the time the crew realized how dull she was, it would be too late to replace her. The best they could hope for would be some contrived triumph when she trekked out after six weeks, bruised and hungry, and raised her arms before the setting sun. She'd take the prize and be done with it all, and *Civilization* would never hear from her again.

"You're kidding." The driver was on the phone again. She sighed when she hung up. "I swear . . ." she said, and then stopped herself. "You good?"

Mara realized the question was for her.

"Yes," she said. "Of course." She scratched her blindfold, letting in a blade of light, and put her hand down quickly.

After a few hours, the truck stopped. The driver led Mara by the elbow, brusquely, across a stretch of gravel; she felt the shape of the rocks through her sandals. A chill in the air. She wished she had a jacket. "Take her," someone said, and then a new hand touched her shoulder, guiding her to a bench. The new hand was tentative. It turned over her arm, gently, and placed a wrapped cheeseburger in her palm.

"I bet you're hungry." A man's voice.

"I guess." Being blindfolded made Mara nauseous, or maybe it was the nerves. In the distance she heard bustling footsteps, voices. The slam of a car door. She unwrapped the burger and took a bite. She wondered if this was her last real meal, but didn't want to ask. She felt hyperaware of every swallow. The lingering salt from the cheese.

"Sorry it's cold," the man said. "We weren't sure when you'd get here." He sat down beside her.

"No, it's fine."

"There's pop, too, if you want it."

When Mara was done eating, she crumpled up the wrapper and felt it plucked from her hand.

There was something in the quality of the man's breath, quiet sighs, that made her think he wanted to talk. She felt he was glancing at her, then glancing away.

"So how'd you get into this?" she said.

"Saw an ad," he said. "Used to work for the local station, back in the day. They wanted someone who didn't mind dirt." He had an accent, but Mara couldn't place it. Loose on the Os.

"So you know the woods here."

"I s'pose."

"Anything I should be prepared for?"

A hesitation. "I'm not supposed to tell you."

"That's okay. We can talk about something else."

"Yeah?"

"Sure. Anything."

"I wanted a change," he said. "That's the thing, you know?"

"A change from what?"

"After my wife left."

"I'm sorry."

"She got with a guy in her dart league. I found out on Valentine's Day. Flowers at the door, but they weren't from me. I said, look, we can work it out. But she wouldn't stay."

"That sucks," said Mara. "It's her loss."

"You think?"

"Of course. Look at you." It was hypothetical; Mara couldn't see him. But she'd hyped up enough nervous clients that it was easy to tweak the script.

"I don't know," he said. "Women say they want a nice guy but I don't know, maybe they don't."

"I think some women do."

"I quit drinking," he said. "I quit chew, too. It saves me eighteen dollars a day. Even my dentist noticed. He said, your teeth look clean, did you quit chew? And I said yes. But she doesn't care. I think women maybe, they just don't like me."

"What kind of women do you like?"

"You know," he said. "Women who want to do things. Or just sit and talk. Like this, you know?"

"Blindfolded?"

He was confused.

"Never mind," said Mara. "It was a joke." She hoped that if she kept the man talking, he'd slip up and say something useful about the show. But instead he went on about his ex-wife for a while, and Mara stopped paying attention, listening just enough to agree at the right moments, to reassure him that he was better off.

The bustling in the distance had stilled. Eventually footsteps approached. Someone told her to stand, then guided her by the arm in a new direction. "Bye," came a voice from behind her, but already it sounded far away.

Hands took off her blindfold. She was in a gravel pit, surrounded by evergreen forest. A few men stood around, talking into radios or checking clipboards. There was a gray helicopter with a red belly, just sitting, like some sort of poisonous frog or bug. Guys with cameras on their shoulders, big, so their faces were hidden. One of them led Mara to the helicopter, where he buckled her into the front seat, beside the pilot. Then came the blindfold again. The pinch and weight of a headset.

For the first time all day, Mara was grateful not to see. She had never loved heights. The rotors woke and soon the helicopter thundered and rose, and it felt like the blood in her veins was rumbling with it.

The air grew colder. She breathed slowly, deep breaths, trying not to shiver. She wondered if the crew was filming her now, somehow. They would probably film her every second of the next six weeks, and maybe then some. It gave her a strange feeling, as if everything she did belonged to someone else.

21

After what seemed like an hour, the rumbling changed, and a voice came through the headset. Shouting in Mara's ears. The pilot.

"You can take off your blindfold." She had a nice voice.

Mara untied the cloth, careful not to nudge the headset and let in more of the deafening noise. There was bright light. Stinging, blinking, until her eyes adjusted. She glanced down to her right and felt sick.

They hovered above a lake, deep blue. Dense forest in all directions—mostly fir, Mara thought, though already she felt uncertain; the evergreens mixed with bare, dense branches she didn't know offhand. It was a clear day, and the pale, almost neon quality of green on the banks suggested late spring, new growth, a landscape not yet tipped into summer. Back in Washington it had been warm for a month.

On the lakeshore Mara saw movement, another cluster of men in pants and windbreakers, and just past them, in a clearing, two figures dressed in brown outfits like hers. One of them shaded their eyes and waved. The other crouched. Mara couldn't tell what they were doing. She waited for the helicopter to fly to the clearing, but it hovered in the air. The wind whipped rings in the water below.

"You have to open your door," said the pilot. She was shouting for the noise, but she said it as casually as one might of a parked car.

"My door?"

The pilot gestured roughly. "Make sure you jump out, not up. If you want to keep your head."

Then Mara understood. The show had begun. She was expected to fall from the helicopter into the lake. She was expected to swim to shore.

She recognized that this was clever of the producer. It would make for a great entrance. She might cry or freeze; already she felt her chest tightening. But beyond the obvious dramatic footage—survivors flinging themselves from the sky—jumping into the lake would up the stakes immediately. They were somewhere north, maybe even boreal, and the night would be cold enough without soaked clothing. Already it was late afternoon. The moment she hit the water, she'd start edging toward hypothermia, and stay at risk until she managed to dry her clothes.

If she thought about the jump, if she prepared for it, she would panic. She unclipped her seat belt, opened the door, and fell.

4

A wailing sound; a wall of sound. And then the punch of frigid water. It slammed the air from Mara's lungs. She sank deep, peaceful into the darkness, until her chest burned, and then in a few strokes she broke the surface. She gasped harder than she intended. Glad that the cameras weren't close.

Already the helicopter had lifted away, and the water, whipped into swells, was starting to calm. Mara spotted land and swam toward it, kicking until her toes touched reeds. A few more kicks and she pulled herself onto the shore. The air was cold, but the muck at the water's edge was warmed slightly from the sun.

Just six weeks and she'd be free.

Mara looked up. Sure enough, two cameramen stood above her. She crawled up the muddy bank, trying to act natural, and stumbled when she rose to her feet. The ground was thick with dead leaves.

A tall man in a white visor stepped forward and shook her hand. Lenny. He squeezed hard. She heard the *whirr* of a camera zooming in.

"Mara," he said. Smooth and deep. "Welcome. You'll meet your teammates shortly. I know you must be eager to get started. But first you have to make a decision."

He led her to a collection of tools and objects, arranged on a cowhide on the grass.

"Think carefully about what you're here for. What you'll need. What you're leaving behind. You can pick one thing to help you on your path."

"Just one?" said Mara.

"Hold on," said a crew member. He stepped forward and clipped a microphone to Mara's collar, feeding the cord through her wet tunic, and tucked the battery pack into a pocket in her shorts. Careful not to touch her skin. He stepped back. "Okay, say it again."

"Just one?" said Mara, stiffly.

"That's right," said Lenny. "Take your pick."

Mara took stock of the options. An axe, a roll of fishing line, a pot with a lid. A dark-handled knife in a leather sheath. A case of waterproof matches. A sleeping bag. A lighter. A large jar of peanut butter. A King James Bible. A phone. A tiny bottle of iodine. A fat brown envelope labeled *$10,000.*

Mara traced her fingers over the sleeping bag, trying not to drip on it. It was small, a summer-weight mummy. Polyester. The phone was obviously a symbol. It was worthless without power or reception.

"The money," she said. "If I take it, what then?"

Lenny smiled. "Whatever you pick is yours to keep."

So this was a test. And a good one. Ten thousand dollars was far more than she'd ever had at once.

It was a matter of confidence, Mara supposed. A gamble: she could pick something that would help her last six weeks in the woods, bring her closer to the real prize money, or she could hedge her bets now. What could she buy with ten grand? A better used car; enough gas to drive far away. But then what? She'd run out eventually. She'd need another job. The envelope was unsealed, and she opened the flap with her thumb, revealing a stack of hundreds. Green and crisp. Her heart beat faster.

She put down the envelope and picked up the knife. It felt good in her hand, cool and smooth. The back of the blade was serrated for sawing. The handle was inlaid with ebony. An artist's work.

"What did the others pick?" she asked.

"This is about you," said Lenny. "It's about your instincts."

"So you won't tell me."

"Their choices shouldn't affect yours," he said, and she felt insulted by the lie. Not that he told it, but that she had to accept it.

Money wouldn't keep her warm and fed. She'd come to make it to the end.

Mara unsheathed the knife and slid the blade up her forearm, watching brown hairs fall loose. She wished she could pick the sleeping bag. And the fishing line, the matches, something to purify water—either the iodine or the pot. They'd need food, fire. A knife would only get her partway there, but what could she really do without one?

Besides. She liked it.

"I've chosen," she said. "I'm ready to meet the others."

But when Lenny led her across the clearing, toward where two men knelt in the dead grass, her heart sank. Because one of them had a machete, which was redundant; how many blades did they need, as a team? And the other held a goddamn bow drill. They were dressed like she was and only slightly less drenched, huddled around a pile of sticks.

Mara took a breath, tried to smile, and dropped to her knees beside them. "Looks like we're building a fire."

"Trying to," said the one with the machete. He was maybe forty, with tan skin and muscular shoulders, like he worked out at a gym. He was a math teacher. That was James.

Kyle was much younger. Red hair and thin arms, constellations of zits. His teeth chattered loudly. He greeted Mara briefly before turning back to the bow drill, which he'd pinned under one freckled knee. He pushed the bow back and forth, but only a tendril of smoke rose from the point of friction. He was shivering so hard that even the smoke wavered.

At Primal Instinct, Mara gave clients a choice in fire-starting classes, letting them pick between a bow drill, flint, magnesium rod, or a single match to start their fires. Everyone chose bow drill, even though it was hardest. *Because* it was hardest. And fickle, which meant, of course, that it should be the last resort in any real situation. Classes were one thing, but if Kyle, with his pick of fire starters, had knowingly grabbed the unreliable one—

"I've done this at home," said Kyle, through clacking teeth. "I can do it, no problem."

"Let me guess," Mara said. "You even made one yourself."

"In Scouts," he said, looking up pleased. When he realized

it wasn't a compliment, he looked back down. Mara felt bad. She didn't mean to be harsh. It just happened sometimes.

"I know a trick," she said. "If you want help."

"I got it." Now Kyle was defensive.

Mara looked around. The meadow was surrounded by trees. Mostly fir and white pine, though at the far edge of the clearing a maple towered above the rest, dead and split at the top. The buzz of insects. Somewhere a crow *caw-caw*ed.

The underbrush was thin, which struck her as promising. She had always liked an airy woods. From a distance she thought she recognized bee balm, and broad leaves that might be violets. Farther on, the terrain rolled into a series of hills, culminating in a mountain a few miles away. To the northwest, judging by the light.

It wasn't a tropical paradise, but it wasn't the worst place, either. Workable. Lush in a modest way, and rustling with birds, the sense of springing branches just out of sight, things living in the trees and in the shadows between them. The temperature was probably midfifties, and cooler in the shade. No breeze. The sun hung two fists' height above the horizon.

A whine sounded, a gnat whine, and grew stronger as the helicopter approached from the south. That deep roar as it stalled, whipping the lake into whitecaps. Waves sighed against the shore. The helicopter door stayed open for a long time. Then someone dropped, and Mara was struck by how quick it was, a pin-straight figure there then gone.

A few minutes later, a sun-creased man with a white beard approached the group, clutching an axe in one hand. He shook himself like a dog, took in the scene, and sniffed.

That was Bullfrog.

"Bow drill?" he said. "Jesus Christ, kid. You're going to

need some fatwood for that." He turned past them into the trees, swinging the axe over his shoulder. James, seeming grateful for the excuse, stood and followed.

So at least one of Mara's new teammates had sense.

Now she was alone with Kyle, or kind of alone. He was shivering harder. Glancing at the cameras. She might have felt for him if she weren't so cold herself. The sun was only teasing now. Without a fire they'd have to walk all night for warmth.

"Hey," said Mara. She tried to make her voice gentle. "Seriously, I know a trick for the bow drill. Could I just give it a try?" If Kyle thought she was patronizing, he would say no.

"I know how to use it."

"It's a weird trick. We could try it together."

Kyle was intrigued enough that he loosened his grip on the bow, or maybe he was desperate. The notch he'd worn in the base was smooth and black. Mara cut a new one with her knife. She took one end of the bow in her hand and guided his hand to the other.

"Like this," she said. "I push, you pull. And then we switch. Back and forth."

The problem with bow drills was that people's arms got tired before a proper coal had formed. It was easy to lose rhythm at critical moments. But with two people you could share the work, keep the rhythm for longer.

Mara slid the bow, slow and even, until she felt Kyle mirroring her movements. She kept the rhythm steady. Pushing and pulling until smoke billowed around them, stinging their eyes, rising toward the sky. A fire's worth of smoke, invisible flames. It was time.

As soon as Mara let go, Kyle scrambled. He tipped the coal into a nest of shredded birch bark and puffed at it furiously.

Too fast, Mara thought. He could relax. But flames burst from his cupped hands. He dropped the fireball onto twigs and it began to grow.

Bullfrog and James returned with chunks of crumbled fatwood, armloads of sticks, and together they fed the crackling flames. Mara leaned back and watched them. Already she felt her tunic growing crisp in the waves of heat. Pulling the chill from her bones.

When they heard the engine again, they all watched it come.

A figure appeared in the helicopter doorway, silhouetted against the sunset. In one movement she dove from the sky, vanishing without a splash into the rings of water. Soon she stood by the fire, dripping and grinning. She set a pot on the ground before them. Then she gathered her hair over one shoulder and wrung it in a thick twist. "I'm Ashley," she said. "Nice fire you all have going. I can tell we're gonna get along."

When Ashley looked at her, Mara felt a shock, as if she'd hit the cold water once more. And then Ashley looked away and the moment broke, and Mara knew it was hers alone. She had imagined it—she must have, because it made no sense to feel like that. She put the shock from her mind and held her palms to the flames.

NOW THAT THEY WERE ALL TOGETHER, AND WOULD NOT FREEZE, LENNY CAME TO THE fire for a talk. The survivors sat in a ring like children, and he stood above them. Mara tried not to look at Ashley. She tried to look interested and calm.

"Welcome to *Civilization*," said Lenny. "As you know, I'm your producer. And your host. This show is kind of my baby, which makes you all, well . . ." He chuckled. "Anyway, the point of the challenge is to see what happens when a team of survivors"—here he pointed at each of them in turn—"are given freedom to rebuild society from the ground up. You're strangers to each other. You come from different backgrounds. But each of you is here for a reason. We see something special in every one of you."

A camera guy, creeping backward, tripped on a root and squeaked. Lenny cleared his throat.

"Remember," he continued, "this is a new kind of show. It's a competition, but you're competing together. Everyone who makes it to the end wins." There was an incantatory quality to his voice that suggested he had practiced the lines, but it was subtle. He had practiced well. "You don't have to worry about rules. You *make* the rules. You can hunt, fish, cut down trees, whatever you want and need. You can build a skyscraper! Whatever you dream about. It's yours. Although"—he paused for a second and touched his ear; he was getting a message through an earpiece—"we do ask that you don't eat rabbits."

"They're protected?" said James.

"No," said Lenny. "But the network has a thing for rabbits. I guess if you catch one, we won't stop you, but we probably won't film it."

"Also," said Kyle, "rabbits carry tularemia, and we don't have access to soap for proper sanitation."

Mara could have sworn that Bullfrog rolled his eyes.

"So we agree," said Lenny. He went on to cover logistics that Mara already knew, or had assumed. Survivors would not be provided food or water, nor replacement clothing, so they should care for what they had. If they changed their appearance they should do so on film, for the sake of continuity. The crew would come and go throughout the day; at night they went to their own camp nearby. They were not to speak to the survivors, though survivors could talk to the cameras whenever they chose. "There are cameras in the trees, too, and you're welcome to interact with them—share your worries, show off something you made. Think of them as your personal confidants."

Now Lenny adjusted his visor and shifted his weight. "One more thing. If you have your period, ladies—is anyone on their period?"

Mara let herself look at Ashley. She could feel the men trying not to look at either of them.

Ashley raised her hand slightly.

"Cool," said Lenny. "That's completely cool. Don't worry about it. We have tampons on demand. Just, uh, when you're done with a tampon, give it to me and I'll get rid of it for you."

"You want me to give you my used tampons?"

"Don't be self-conscious," said Lenny. "It's normal. No judgment, okay?"

Ashley looked incredulous, but she shook herself a little, and the look went away in an instant. It was amazing how quickly she readjusted her face.

"Of course," she said. "No problem."

Mara thought they were done, but Kyle and James had questions—should they ask permission before leaving camp, that sort of thing—that went on far too long. Finally Lenny zipped up his coat. "One last thing," he said. "I'd suggest you don't wander too far alone. We have eyes on a bear and her cub, and she's shown some aggression. We're armed, but you're not." Mara wondered if the bear was real, or if there was some other reason he wanted to keep them close. "I mean it," said Lenny, as if he could read her mind. "It's better to watch out."

5

deally, by nightfall at a new camp, Mara would have a shelter built. Something compact for warmth, with good insulation, and more or less watertight. A fire going, and a stockpile of wood: thick logs to burn while she slept, and handfuls of grass and twigs for when she woke and had to wake the coals. Plus water, of course, treated or filtered or boiled.

More than that, she'd have a sense of the area. Animal signs, tracks and trails. Thorny or stinging plants to avoid. If she heard sounds from the darkness, she'd know where the creatures came from and where they were going. She liked to know what surrounded her in the night.

It wasn't a big deal, but she felt put off by not having time to settle in before dark. She blamed Kyle and James for the tedious questions that took up the last half hour of light. There would be endless time for logistics in the next days and weeks, and no way now to make a shelter for the night, or to explore.

But at least they had a fire, and wood to last through morning. Smoke to keep the mosquitos slow. And bright stars above; it didn't look like rain. It could have been better; it could have been worse.

Bullfrog lay down and closed his eyes, and though Mara could have done the same, she was struck with some vague sense of social duty and instead sat up with the others and envied him. The fire crackled pleasantly, and sparks rose toward the sky.

Kyle was griping about the rabbit ban.

"This is survival," he said. "Real survival means using whatever resources you find. That's the whole point of it. You're surviving. Anything goes."

"This isn't survival," said Mara. She wondered how the mic worked. If Lenny was listening to her right now over a radio somehow, or if he would only hear her later.

"Look at us," said Kyle. "Of course it's survival."

"It's a survival game," she said. "We're playing the game. It's not survival if you have a choice."

Kyle looked crestfallen, and Mara felt annoyed. He was too easy to discourage; this was the second time she had hurt his feelings by saying something obvious and true. She would have to watch her words, or risk looking rude on-screen, which would make it hard to be invisible.

"So," said Ashley, saving her. "What are you all here for? I came to get famous. That's the plan, at least." It was so blunt that James laughed, which broke the tension. His laugh echoed in the trees.

Mara must have been more tired than she realized, or just relieved to be off the hook, because she drifted off to the three of them talking about fame and money and adventure. Only bits of the conversation stuck with her. How James ended his semester early, and his students made him cards, but he couldn't talk about the show, so they thought he went on vacation to Guatemala. He planned to buy fake souvenirs online to show them in the fall.

There was something about Chris McCandless, that guy who died in the Alaskan wilds some decades back. How Kyle idolized him. Ashley's laughter, sweet and deep. Something about bridges, and swimming. Something about a wife.

Mara woke at intervals, shivering, to feed the fire and rearrange herself on the dirt, but it was not the worst night she'd spent, and she surprised herself with sleep.

THE SONGBIRDS HAD BARELY STARTED HOLLERING AGAIN WHEN THE CREW CAME back single file, boots squelching in the dew, and started setting up: changing batteries in the static cameras, putting tripods in places where they thought the survivors might be interesting. They murmured together in short bursts, but Mara could not make out the words. She counted six crew members plus Lenny, all men, all wearing windbreakers. One of them, a blond guy, showed the survivors how to change the batteries in their mics. He hid a case of fresh batteries behind a log so they could do it themselves each morning.

The survivors couldn't have slept much longer anyway. They were damp, and the firewood was spent. Bullfrog announced that he'd build a shelter and would rather not have help—bless him for saying that out loud, Mara thought—and so while the other three discussed water, she took the chance to slip into the woods.

She had spotted a creek from the air, west of the clearing,

and she thought she might find horsetails there. Late spring was lousy for foraging, but there was always food if you knew where to look. Young shoots from plants that would be tough by June and bitter by July. Ramps and pine tips. Fiddleheads before they uncurled. The mossy ground was dry and coarse, almost spongelike. Green leaves poked through it like spears, and white flowers grew in such thick patches that they looked like dustings of snow. But last year's dead beech leaves still clung to branches, fluttering, translucent. It gave the woods an odd effect, as if it were spring below and autumn above, as if the seasons rose from the earth in layers rather than descending from the sky.

Mara waved a stick to knock away spiderwebs, though a few loose strands still clung to her face. She heard steps and froze; she thought she had lost the cameras. What kind of performance did they want from her? She touched a spruce tree, then plucked off a few pine needles and sniffed them. She tried to look purposeful and wise. But after a few minutes she heard a commotion back at camp, which must have been more important than she was, because the footsteps turned back and she was mercifully alone.

She followed a game trail, the sound of burbling, and found the creek quickly. It was wide and shallow with short, steep banks. Thick roots eddied the current, and gliders skidded at the smooth edges, casting shadows on the minnows that gleamed in the light.

Mara crouched and dipped her fingers in the water. There were deer tracks in the half-hardened mud, and smaller prints—raccoon maybe, or skunk. The water was gold from the tannins of old leaves, with a surface like silk ribbons. Better for drinking than the mucky water of the lake.

Something rustled behind her, and she froze again. Another camera. Did it make sense to touch the water? Was this, too, a performance? But this time the steps came closer.

"Don't say anything." Barely a whisper.

When Mara turned, he pressed a finger to his mouth.

It was one of the camera guys, a thin man in faded jeans, but his hands were empty. He glanced over his shoulder, then pointed to a distant grove of birch.

Mara followed him to the birch grove, out of sight of the creek. The sun through the leaves cast mottled shadows on his face. He touched her hip and she stiffened, but he had only flicked off her mic.

"How are you doing?" he said quietly. "How was your night?"

Mara tried to recall if they'd met.

"It's me," he said. "Tom. I gave you a burger. We talked in the gravel pit?"

"With the ex-wife?"

Tom broke into a grin. Now Mara felt oddly relieved to see him. Someone from before this place, though of course they had only met yesterday.

"It's nice here," she said. "These are gorgeous woods."

Tom liked that. She knew he would. "And the other survivors?" he asked.

Mara shrugged.

"The men treating you right?"

"Bullfrog seems like he has some skills."

Tom snorted. "Most of the crew bet he lasts the longest," he said, and then he caught himself. "But I didn't like the way they were talking. I told them. I put my money on you."

"I hope I can earn a return on your investment."

"It's not about that."

"I'm teasing. It's fine."

"It's a good thing you have me." He touched a hand to a holster on his waist. "Someone to watch your back. You never know up here."

"Do you always carry in the woods?"

Tom grinned. Mara wondered how he might fancy himself. Chivalrous, watching a lady, when all she needed was to be more closely watched. But if he was talking to her, if he set his camera down, it meant he was willing to bend the rules, too. It might be good to have someone like that on her side.

"Well," said Mara. "I'm glad you're here."

"Of course," he said. Not breaking her gaze. "I think you're special, Mara."

"I don't know about that."

"I do. I can see it. Look, I have to go. Don't tell anyone we talked, okay?" He flicked her mic back on, tapped his heart twice, and slipped away.

IF MARA HAD KNOWN THE SHOW'S LOCATION IN ADVANCE, SHE WOULD HAVE STUDIED the plants. In a week's time she could have memorized the staples. But as she searched the woods, she grew frustrated. Many of the leaves she saw were unfamiliar, or too young to identify with confidence. She found several clumps of fiddle-heads, but they were fuzzy, a species of fern she didn't know. She could have touched them to her wrist, to her tongue, to check for a reaction. But she didn't feel like waiting or getting sick, and so with reluctance she let them be.

If they had arrived a few weeks earlier, when the nights sank below freezing, she could have tapped maple trees, and she fell into a brief daydream about how she might have done it without a drill or metal spiles. She had never tapped maple back home, but she knew the concept and thought there must be a simple way with wooden tools. She'd heard that you could tap birch trees, too, but they gave less sap, and anyway it was a moot point this late in the season.

Finally she found a patch of sumac shoots, which she recognized from the taller bushes around them, their long leaves. The shoots were crisp and broke easily, the center stalks thick as her pinkie. She ate several and then gathered the rest in her tunic to bring to camp.

On the walk back she felt a presence, and froze once more, but it was only a deer. They stared at each other unblinking. Then the deer turned, white tail flashing as it bounded through the woods, and Mara saw that it had been browsing a stand of wood nettles, barely a foot tall and tufting at the tops with still-curled leaves. She felt grateful for the deer, because she might not have noticed the young plants without it, and as she walked back, thinking of nettle tea and nettle soup, she almost forgot she was in a show.

The reprieve didn't last long. Back at camp, Lenny was arranging promotional photographs, portraits of each survivor. He tapped Bullfrog for a photo first, which was a bold move, because Mara got the sense he wouldn't be big on publicity. But what did she know? Bullfrog had come here, after all. He must have cooperated well enough, because Mara glimpsed him through the trees, posing square-legged with his arms crossed, white beard shining in the sun.

"How about this?" Kyle practiced poses while Ashley humored him.

"Try bending your knee more," she said. "Lift your chin."

She steered him into a crouched position that actually looked good. Reserved but agile, coiled, as if he might spring up at any time. More scrappy than skinny.

"My turn," said Ashley. "I'm going to try three poses. Tell me which one is best."

Mara looked around. Ashley was talking to both of them.

"Okay," said Mara. She sat down by the fire.

"Here's the first." Ashley stood with a wide stance, legs locked, and put her hands on her hips. Looked out at the distance, lifted her chin.

"Wonder Woman," said Kyle.

"You look strong," said Mara. She thought that her feedback was better than Kyle's.

"All right," said Ashley. "Strong is good. That's one option."

Next she knelt by the fire, beside Mara; Mara wondered if she should move away. Ashley held the pot out over the flames, as if she were setting it there to boil, or else retrieving it. She posed for a few seconds and then withdrew her arm, laughing. "I can't hold this for long. I'll burn myself. But you get the idea."

"Eh," said Kyle, politely.

"I like it," said Mara. "I like that it shows you doing something."

Ashley nodded. "Doing something. Got it."

For her last pose, she stood, smiling, and held out the pot with both hands. As if offering a drink. And Mara was struck by how simple it was—a pot—and how annoying it would be to survive without it, and how none of the others, even her, would have picked something quite so useful and plain.

"Definitely go with Wonder Woman," said Kyle.

"I like the last one best," said Mara.

"Why?" Ashley put the pot down.

"It seems more like you. Friendly. You didn't come here to be tough, right? You came to connect with people."

"That's the one I liked," said Ashley. "I'm glad you don't think it's stupid."

"None of them are stupid."

"The first pose seems powerful, though," said Kyle. Ashley just smiled. The decision was made.

But when it came time for Ashley's photos, Lenny directed her to the lake instead. He wanted to capture her rising from the water.

"It'll be great," he said. "You're a swimmer, right?"

"In high school," said Ashley. "Are you sure? I like holding the pot."

"I'll be honest with you, Ash. It's not about the pot."

"I thought I could hold it out to the camera."

"Look at the light," Lenny said. "The way it's angled right now. You'll look great."

Ashley followed him to the shore.

Mara watched as Ashley took off her sandals and walked into the lake waist-deep. Ducked under and rose up, again and again, tunic stuck to her body, light glinting off her wet skin. Soon she was shivering. Lenny told her to swim around and come back when she was warm.

As soon as Ashley turned from shore, Mara saw what she meant about being a swimmer. Ashley slipped through the water like it was nothing, like she was pulled by an unseen string. Mara heard a twig crack and looked away—it was Bull-frog, dragging a log and grunting—and when she turned back to the lake a moment later, Ashley had almost reached the far shore.

She'd be cold when she got out. For that matter, so would Mara, if Lenny put her in the lake next. She added new wood to the fire, a thick branch, and broke sticks in pieces to add them, too. Soon the flames rose, the breath of it hot on her skin.

By the time Ashley came back, the fire was roaring, and she knelt down beside it. "Thank you," she said, and Mara felt too warm. She backed up a few steps.

Anyway, it turned out Lenny didn't want Mara in the lake. He asked her to stand simply, one hand to her chest, and gaze at the horizon. In five minutes she was done.

By evening, Bullfrog had the frame of a lean-to built: two tripods made of thin birch trunks, with a beam set between them, and smaller poles laid against one side for shade. It would not hold warmth yet, or stop rain, but the structure itself was comforting. The survivors sat in a row beneath it, beside the fire. They had all gathered firewood, and the pile of branches beside them was comforting, too.

Mara boiled sumac shoots with nettle leaves to make a watery soup, which would have been well served by the additions of salt and heavy cream. It was bitter, and some of the greens turned mucosal in the heat. Still, she and her teammates passed the pot, taking swigs and scooping wet leaves with their fingers. When the soup cooled, Mara placed it back on the coals, and the flavor improved upon reheating. Even by firelight the broth shone green.

Mara felt okay. Hungry, but she'd be hungrier soon, and grateful the gnats were lethargic. The sun was stronger than at home, and her cheeks felt puffy and raw. Sunburn. Foolish not to anticipate. Maybe she could find something, mud or ashes, to shield her skin tomorrow.

She expected to sleep better that night, with the frame of the shelter and, more importantly, a sense of her surroundings. But she woke, freezing, to movement. James beside her, sitting bolt upright. The whites of his eyes shone in the firelight.

"Did you hear that?" he said.

Mara had heard any number of sounds since dusk. Twigs and wind, buzzing insects. The yips of coyotes from three directions. Splashes from the lake. She listened awhile, but heard nothing new. In fact it was oddly quiet.

"It's just the woods," she said. "Go back to sleep."

But James didn't move.

"There it is," he said. "I heard it again."

Sometimes people freaked out at Primal Instinct. Positive they'd heard footsteps or voices. Often they had. There were always things in the night. Approaching, watching, slipping away. Mara took rustles for granted. The woods were someone else's house. People weren't guests; they were intruders.

"I don't like this," said James.

"I think we're fine."

"You don't know that. You don't know what happens when you're asleep."

"If I'm asleep," she said, "it doesn't matter."

"I disagree."

Mara shrugged. The night was moonless, black, and the dark pressed from all sides. The fire's glow a small and flickering ring.

"Maybe we can take shifts," James said. "Sitting up and keeping guard."

"I'm not worried about it. I'm going back to sleep."

He didn't respond.

Mara lay down, but she watched James for a while. She wished he would relax. He made her more nervous than the darkness did. When she closed her eyes she could still see him, alert and silhouetted. In her dreams, he sat there all night.

6

On the second morning, Lenny came singing. Mara heard his voice from a distance and the crash of the crew that followed. Their footsteps seemed unnaturally heavy, until she remembered that the crew wore boots while the survivors were basically barefoot. As if animals weren't already avoiding them; as if there was any possibility of sneaking up on prey. Not that hunting was Mara's specialty, or that she had a weapon prepared, but she imagined she'd have a chance if the crew weren't blasting a parade through the whole forest. Lenny was still whistling when he reached the fire.

"Guys," he said. "Listen. Normally I won't help you like this, so don't get used to it. But I have a tip for you."

It was cramped in the lean-to, and Mara needed to stretch, but she didn't want to touch the others. She crawled onto the damp grass.

"You know that mountain there?" said Lenny. The survivors did, of course, but he waited until they looked before he continued. He didn't just expect attention, Mara thought, but performance. In every way.

"One of the guys did some scouting," Lenny said. "And you'll never guess what he found."

"What did he find?" said Kyle.

"Alpine strawberries. A whole slope of them, just ripe. And it's supposed to be clear all day. Consider this information a gift from me to you."

"I'll go," said James. "Is that all right? Can I go?"

Mara couldn't tell who he was asking. She was already thinking about the taste of berries.

"Maybe there should be two of you," said Lenny.

"I'll go with him," said Ashley.

"It's farther than it looks," said Kyle. "I don't know if it's worth the calories."

"Not everything is about calories," said Ashley. "Some things are about fun."

If Mara said that, Kyle would be defensive. But with Ashley he just grinned.

"We can scout along the way," said James. "Get a real sense of the area. It'll be useful."

"You should bring the pot," Mara said. There was a silence, as if she'd said something confusing. "The pot of water. I mean, Ashley, I know it's yours. But you should bring it to drink from. The rest of us can go without."

"It's not really mine," she said. "We're sharing our tools, right?"

Bullfrog sniffed.

The pot had a little broth left from the night before, just a slosh in the bottom, murky with ashes. Mara drank it in one gulp. "That's good for me," she said. "I'll boil more water, and Kyle and Bullfrog can drink it. And then I'll boil one more for you to bring with you. Give me forty minutes."

While the others discussed routes up the mountain, how to avoid rockfalls and steer for the gentle spine, Mara went to the lake. Somewhere a turtle splashed. She waded in, but her feet raised muck from the bottom, so she waited for it to settle before filling the pot.

The fire had dwindled overnight and the coals were low; it took some time for the water to heat up. Mara pushed coals around the pot until flames licked every side. Once it had boiled, she lifted the sizzling pot with a branch and dipped it back in the lake to cool it. It sent up a hiss of steam. Kyle and Bullfrog drank their fill, and she did it all again.

It wasn't much water to go on for the day, for any of them. Mara figured they were already dehydrated. In fact, now that she thought more about it, the whole mountain plan seemed unnecessary, and she half regretted encouraging Ashley to take the pot. If she'd known yesterday that they'd be splitting up, she could have burned out a wooden bowl to store drinking water in camp, too.

Hubbub as the crew prepared. Cameras were hoisted; batteries switched out. Lenny filmed James and Ashley talking as if the trip had been their idea.

"I have a hunch," said James. "Call it intuition. I saw that mountain and I thought: there's gonna be strawberries up there. And probably a whole lot."

"If we pick enough," Ashley told the camera, "it'll make a big difference for us. We can dry them and store them long-term."

"We want to provide for our team," said James.

Then they left with the pot and Lenny followed and everything was still after that.

Mara considered her options for the morning. She could go back and harvest more nettles, whose stinging hairs were weak this early in the year. If she scraped the stems with bits of bark, they could even be eaten raw, and she could dry plenty of leaves for tea. Bullfrog would work on the shelter, and Kyle would whatever, and when the others came back from the mountain they'd have a meal of berries and tea and stalks.

But first things first. Mara went to the fire and found the smoothest ashes and dabbed them on her face. Something to block the sun at least, and keep the burn from getting worse. On second thought, she took another handful of ashes and rubbed them into her arms and legs. The ashes were white, almost feathery, and melted like velvet into her skin, casting her limbs a pale gray.

She sensed that someone was near her, watching and filming, but she didn't look up. What had Lenny said about continuity? If they changed their appearance, it needed to be on film. Well, she thought, here I am, turning gray. Knock yourselves out.

A pair of legs, leather boots, walked past her, and something fell to the ground at her side. As if by instinct, Mara stretched and shifted, putting her hand over the object. It was a twig, smooth and pale. Birch.

After a few minutes, she announced to no one that she had to pee, stood from the fire, brushed the loosest ashes from her forearms, and walked casually into the woods. She found Tom by the birch grove, sitting on a log with the camera on his lap. He pressed a button on the camera and its light flickered off. Set it down on the ground, facing away. She switched off her mic. Now they were really alone.

"I wanted to check in," he said. "While the others are gone. How are you?"

"Good, I guess. I got some sun."

"It's stronger here than folks realize."

"I see that now."

"I brought you something."

"Oh," said Mara. "Thank you."

"But you can't tell anyone. I could lose my job."

"I won't tell," she said.

"I'm serious. No one can know."

Mara looked around; there were no other cameras in the trees. She figured Tom wanted stakes to bring them together, a cause to make his life interesting. He was being so dramatic. She hoped he had something good.

"You can trust me," she said, sitting down on the log beside him. Not close, but not far. "I won't say a word. We would both get in trouble."

Tom liked that. He pressed his fingers together, as if weighing the odds.

"You can trust me," she repeated softly.

"I know I can," he said. "I could tell that about you right away."

He reached into his pocket and handed her a protein bar.

Mara's mouth filled with water. She hadn't eaten more than leaves in almost two days, and was hungrier than she wanted to admit. She wanted to be alone, to have privacy for the pleasure that eating would entail, but Tom didn't leave. He took the bar from her—her heart fell—then tore the wrapper open and handed it back.

The flesh of the bar was dark brown, almost purple, made of some matte and hardened goo. The smell of peanuts. Mara bit off a corner with her teeth. As if on cue, her stomach rumbled.

Tom watched her chew.

Mara couldn't decide whether to eat fast or slow, so she settled in the middle. Chewing big bites for too long, then swallowing in gulps, feeling them sink down her throat. In six bites, the bar was gone. Somehow she felt hungrier than before. She wanted another. She wanted fries and a hot ham sandwich.

Tom held out his hand, and Mara gave him back the wrapper. He folded it in a neat square and tucked it in his breast pocket.

"I can do this for you," he said. "Maybe not every day. But I want you to stay strong."

"Thank you," said Mara, and meant it. Hunger, even two days' hunger, brought its own humility. If being Tom's project meant extra food, it was humility she could live with.

When Tom left, she didn't go back to camp right away. She could hear Kyle and Bullfrog arguing in the distance. Something about shelter; the louder voice was Kyle's. Anyway, they might smell the peanuts on her breath. She decided instead to explore.

She followed the creek upstream. It was easier to walk through the water than around it, and she took careful steps, feeling with her toes, occasionally stepping off ledges that left her thigh-deep and soaked the hem of her shorts. The water was soothing, numbing. It raised wakes around her legs.

Before long, the creek widened and curved sharply around a bar of gravel, thirty feet long, with a few thin trees fallen across it. Mara climbed onto the stones and found a piece of quartz that she set on a log before continuing on. The creek led to the right and through a stand of pine before reaching another sunlit clearing. The water broke over shallow rapids, then smoothed, and a few hardy bubbles floated downstream.

Content that the ashes protected her skin, and that she was finally unwatched, Mara lay down in the sun and closed her eyes.

She woke to a shadow over her face. By the time she remembered where she was, the shadow had passed. It took her a moment to figure out what had cast it.

A few feet away, a bear watched her sit up. The bear was not familiar with humans; she had come, curious, to investigate, with her cub tumbling behind.

The bear had a strong smell. Like fish and blood, heavy in the air, and Mara thought that maybe she had noticed this smell in the woods before and not known the source. How many bears had she passed at close range in her life? Now she would know when she did. Mara didn't feel scared, but her heart raced, and goose bumps rose on her arms.

The bear hopped oddly, from one foot to another, and swung her body to turn away. Now Mara saw her cub, loose and careless. He was half-grown, with shoulders as high as his mother's chest. His ears looked too big for his head. The cub had never learned caution. He took a step toward the stranger. Then Mara's stomach rumbled and he backed away.

Mara stayed frozen. After some time the bears decided she was dull, and wandered off in search of mice. Mara waited until her heart had slowed. She walked down the creek, but quickly. The water pushed her along.

Back at camp, Bullfrog wove pine boughs into the lean-to,

and Kyle arranged firewood into stacks of even size. He kept trying to get Bullfrog to chat.

"So you're a hunter," said Kyle.

Bullfrog took a long time to answer. "I'm a meat hunter."

"What's that?"

"It means I hunt out my window for meat."

"But that's illegal, isn't it?"

Bullfrog sighed deeply and reached for another bough.

"I saw a bear," said Mara. "And her cub. A ways up the creek. Just so you know to keep an eye out."

"Most bears aren't dangerous," said Kyle. "They're more afraid of you than you are of them."

"I didn't say I was scared. I said we should be careful. Lenny was right about the bear." Mara thought of the smells of their camp. Smoke and bodies and plants; nothing too appealing. She licked her lips.

She wished Kyle would leave so she could sit by the fire without him, but clearly he wasn't going to. So instead she went to the lakeside and pulled up reeds, beating them with a stick until the stems frayed into fibers. The ends curled like hands, little fists, and then relaxed into strands once more. Mara wound them tightly, twisting between her fingers and thumbs to form a single pliable strand. That was one lesson she knew well for survival: when in doubt, make string.

7

By late afternoon Mara's mouth felt sticky with dry saliva, and as the light slid down the horizon, with no sign of Ashley or James, she started to wonder if she'd drink at all that night. She wished she had kept the pot lid back at camp, if only to boil tiny scoops of water at a time, but she supposed that then Ashley would have nothing to keep the pot from spilling as she walked, and the whole thing would be worse all around. Still, it was bad to get messed up this early in the game, and for a relatively needless reason. She hoped the strawberries were worth it.

Just as Mara had resigned herself to a waterless night, the sound of voices came through the trees, and two figures in brown stumbled into the clearing. Behind them, Lenny and his cameras tromped more loudly than ever, as if they were too weary for even their usual halfhearted finesse.

All Mara could think about was the taste of water. She took the pot from Ashley's hands and made her way in half darkness to the lake's edge, dipping before the muck had even settled. By the time she got back to the shelter, to the fire, the crew was already gone.

In the firelight, James and Ashley wilted. Red lines on their arms and cheeks, hives down their legs. They carried nothing. No berries. Mara saw immediately. But Kyle kept asking, even as they shook their heads.

"Those motherfuckers," said James. "Those motherfuckers."

"Calm down," said Bullfrog, in his deep voice, but even then it took a while for James to really talk.

It seemed that he and Ashley had set out strong, but the mountain was farther away than it looked, and the route, without hard-soled shoes or a cleared trail, steep and slow going. They clambered over boulders and rotten logs. When the overgrowth grew thicker, James wondered aloud how they'd carry the berries back through conditions like this, if it was even worth trying to find them. But each time they discussed turning back, Lenny encouraged them. Saying, "Just wait, you'll see. It'll be fantastic. Trust me," until they had gone so far that they couldn't stand to give up, so far that any step now would get them to the acres of berries, and the thought of fruit in their mouths kept them going, the promise of sugar and moisture and taste.

Exhausted and hungry, they climbed the mountain, one slope after another. Until they reached the very top. It was windy, and the wind was cold. And you know what was there? Stone and moss and scraggly trees. Nothing. As good as nothing.

But still they crawled around, searching, while the crew filmed from every angle. While Lenny asked how it felt to be so wrong. Whether they had let the others down. They filmed

James cursing, and Ashley crying, on top of the mountain in a swirling wind, with lakes and forests spreading endless all around them. A panorama, a killer shot, until all they could do was start the long journey back.

The descent was hard, the slopes crumbly with scree, and the pair was shivering. Their feet bled at the edges, where their sandals didn't protect them. And all for a worthless trick.

"He set us up," said James. "He'd never been up there. He just thought it would make for good footage. Like we're fucking puppets. And he made us look like fools."

Kyle leaned forward, his mouth slightly open. Ashley drew lines in the dirt with her fingers. Mara wondered how she felt.

"Ashley?" she said.

"Yeah," said Ashley. "I suppose." Then she seemed to realize that it wasn't a question. She pushed her fingers deeper in the dirt.

Lenny's trick seemed predictable, in retrospect, and Mara was surprised she had not realized it before. Strawberries bloomed early, but not this early, and not on the colder slopes. But the survivors would grow weaker with time, steadily and soon, and in the next days or weeks the promise of berries might not be enough to lure weary bodies up a mountain. If Lenny wanted footage from the mountaintop, he'd been clever to get it now.

"We could have gotten really hurt," James said. "You should have seen how steep it was. Parts of it. They probably wanted us to fall." His voice rose. "Then they could say, 'Wow, what a shame. What a shame the danger they put themselves in.' I could have broken my leg, or my fucking neck, and they'd stand there and film it, and everyone would think it was because of my own fucking idea."

Eventually he seemed to calm down enough to stop talking, or maybe his anger surpassed the capacity of his words. Mara thought he was overreacting. You see a mountain, and you climb it—that's nobody else's fault. Even if they told you to. You're the one who climbed.

Each time Mara woke that night—many times; the air was cold, and something kept tickling her leg—James stared wide-eyed into the darkness. Just like the night before. And in the morning, when the crew returned, he picked up where he had left off. Like he'd been waiting, or spent the night choosing his words.

"Hey, Lenny," he said. "Lenny. Lenny. I was just wondering. I've been sitting here wondering, what do you think of the ethics of this whole thing?"

Lenny tucked a strand of hair into his visor. "The what?"

"The ethics." James steadied his voice. "You say this is a survival show. But this stuff we're doing, it's not survival. You take our time and our energy with stunts and photo shoots, and we could be spending that time hunting. Or gathering firewood. Or taking a fucking nap. So I'm thinking, if you want us to be survivors, let us make our own decisions. If you want us to be actors, feed us. If I'm exhausted today, and it hurts to walk, it's not because of my skills or my instincts. It's because you set me up to fail. But I'm the one with the consequences. I'm the one who goes another day without eating. I'm the one who looks like a fool in front of the whole fucking world."

Lenny gestured for the nearest camera to come closer. He turned to the rest of the survivors. "I think your teammate might need some help calming down."

Ashley was whispering. Maybe she'd been whispering the whole time.

"It's okay," she said to James. "So we didn't find berries. That's okay. They got the footage they needed. We just won't do it again."

"They lied," he said.

"Maybe not. Maybe Lenny thought there really were strawberries."

"He made it up so we'd do something dangerous," said James. "Sure, maybe he thought there was a chance. But he also knew it didn't matter, because there was nothing we could do about it if he was wrong."

That seemed plausible enough that nobody said anything for a while.

When Ashley spoke again, her voice cracked, like she was already bracing for the response.

"It's okay if you don't want to do this," she said. "You can go home."

James started to cry. His back shook, and he sucked in air with a gulping sound, high-pitched, like he couldn't get enough of it. Like he couldn't get it out of his lungs fast enough, either. It made Mara uncomfortable. She wished he would stop.

Kyle looked away sharply, like someone had dropped their robe. Ashley was bravest of all, because she scooted close and put her hand on James's huge shoulder.

"No one would think less of you," she said. "I promise."

James was sobbing now, clenched forward. Wiping snot on his wrist. A thin whine came out of him, which broke apart into hiccups. Finally he pulled himself together. Heavy swallows, choking a little before he spoke. His voice was low. Like he was talking just to her, or to none of them at all.

"I can't afford to," he said. "We need the prize money. My wife needs . . ." He swallowed again. "I can't afford to leave."

None of the rest of them had much to say about that. They needed the money, too.

MARA WENT TO THE LAKE AND POUNDED REEDS FOR A WHILE. BUT SOMETHING MUST have changed, because when she got back, James was preparing to leave. The survivors sat with their teammate, although he wasn't really their teammate anymore. Two cameras hovered close. One of them was Tom. Mara didn't look at him.

"What about the money?" said Mara. She felt relieved to see him go. James was a lot.

"I need it," said James. "But I don't trust this. You guys will probably be fine, I'm not saying that. But I'm not going to die for reality TV."

"Nobody's dying," said Ashley.

"I know," he said. "But it's not impossible, you know?"

Dying was always possible. Mara wasn't sure what his point was.

James made a show of giving away his machete. Holding it out to Ashley with two hands. "I want you to have this," he said, like it wouldn't be the biggest dick move to take it with him, although of course the cameras loved the scene. "I hope it helps you get through this. All of you." And back to Ashley: "You've got this. I know you do."

Mara didn't like how he talked to her, like they had some long past, when they'd basically hiked together for a day. But Ashley nodded solemnly. She knew her line. Her line was to touch his cheek.

"Maybe you can mail it back to me when you're done," he said. "Obviously use it until then, but if I could get it back afterward . . . It's a nice machete." He asked if Lenny could give Ashley his address, which Lenny promised to do, and just when the whole goodbye seemed like it might drag on forever, Lenny said it was time for him to leave. James hesitated.

"On second thought," he said, "maybe it's better if I take the machete. It would just be easier."

Ashley's eyes flared slightly, but she handed the knife back.

"Good luck," said James. "Stay in touch."

And then he was gone.

Afterward, the survivors had to talk to Lenny about James leaving. They were brought across the meadow one at a time, so they couldn't hear each other.

"What do you think it means that James left?" Lenny asked Mara. "Is this a setback for your team?"

"He wanted to go home," she said.

"Full sentences," said a camera guy. "Present tense."

"I think James just wants to go home," said Mara, and a thumbs-up appeared to let her know she'd done it right.

"Would you say he's weaker than you?"

"He wasn't . . ." Mara said, and then she corrected herself. "I don't think James is weaker than the rest of us." Even as she said them, she became aware of the words *James is weaker* contained in the statement, how an unscrupulous editor could clip out the rest of the sentence, and she wished she could pull the words back in. Not that it mattered, really. Mara was un-impressed with James—not because he went home in under three days, but because of all the agonizing about it. Still, she saw now how it could go if she left, if she had to leave. How they'd ask the others about her, baiting them. Build a story, using her, that wasn't about her at all.

Maybe James's mistrust had rubbed off on her. Or if not his mistrust, his trust. The fact that at first, at least, he had thought things would be transparent and fair.

"I didn't take the bait," she said later, in the shelter. She was glad to say it out loud. It was warm, and they sat at the edge of the shade, four figures in a line on the flattened grass. Bullfrog stretched his hairy toes in the sun.

It felt like someone was missing, which surprised Mara, because it wasn't like she had known James well. And he wasn't missing. He had chosen to leave. People weren't missing when they were where they wanted to be.

"Did Lenny try to get you to say he's weak?" she asked.

"Yeah," said Ashley. "I didn't say it. I could be next, you know?"

It had become clear over three days that Ashley had the least survival experience of all of them. She had poor instincts with fire, putting damp wood on dark coals, blocking the flow of air by accident. She said most of her outdoors experience was car camping. Mara liked that she didn't pretend otherwise. She respected Ashley as much for that as she would for expertise. It struck her as brave both to come here without training and to admit it.

"What about you guys?" said Mara.

Bullfrog, still stretching his toes, gave a nod.

Kyle didn't answer. They all looked at him. Eventually he noticed them looking.

"James was weak," said Kyle. "Objectively. That's not rude to say. It's the truth. It was too much for him."

The light caught his hair, gave it a golden glow, and he

seemed in the moment like a child. An idiot child. But Mara felt a strange protectiveness, which surprised her, and she didn't quite like the feeling. Kyle was annoying, but he was part of the team. Which meant that she was, too, she guessed. Four people on the inside of something no one else would ever truly see.

8

I f there was ever a routine at camp, it was those first days after James left. Though the days made up, proportionately, a tiny portion of the survivors' stay, it was the time that would serve as quintessential, and in retrospect idyllic. Mara did not enjoy the days nearly as much as she would later miss them.

Lenny offered no more missions, and anyway, the survivors probably would not have followed them. Instead he hovered around, directing the cameras and making pointed statements—"I bet you're getting hungry out here"—until somebody, usually Kyle, humored him by repeating them: "You know, I'm really starting to get hungry." The survivors settled on tasks themselves. Bullfrog's shelter grew stronger and more intricate by the hour, bark shingles over layers of moss insulation, with mounds of dry grass and leaves to soften the floor. He built out the shelter's sides until it was less of a lean-to and more of a building in its own right. A slit for the door, which the survivors slipped through sideways, and a fire pit that vented through a hole in the roof. Lenny propped a camera inside, in the far corner. Kyle carved lines in the eave to count the days.

Inside, with the fire, the shelter was much warmer than the outside air, and the survivors no longer shivered in their sleep. They slept curled in chosen quadrants; there was no room to stretch out. But apart from the itchiness of the grass, and the bugs that crawled from the fire and over their bodies, the nights weren't bad. When the morning warmed and the crew arrived, the survivors built a second fire outside, too, so as not to make the shelter too hot. Bullfrog took breaks from building to chop and stack logs faster than they could burn them.

They all did their share of hauling wood, stomping branches to break them and dragging them back to camp. At first they each built their own firewood piles, a competition, and Kyle's pile grew to remarkable height before Mara realized he was gathering wood from around the clearing and not the deeper forest.

"You should get wood from farther away first," she told him. "We'll be here a long time. Save the closer stuff for when we lose strength."

"I don't plan on losing strength," said Kyle.

But Mara wondered if he already had, because rather than gathering distant firewood, he promptly sat down by the lake instead. There he turned his attention to the sedentary task of building traps, whittling en masse the tedious and delicate trigger mechanisms of figure-four deadfalls. The traps were sized to crush small rodents, and each one required three perfectly balanced sticks that supported each other through interlocking notches but crumbled at the lightest touch.

The cameras loved this process, and circled while Kyle worked. "I'm going to get protein for my team," Mara heard him say. Lenny asked about the importance of protein for survival, and Kyle launched into a speech that Mara did her best to ignore. He had her knife and she thought about asking for it back, just to be petty, but reminded herself it was not really hers but theirs, and besides she had other things to do.

She was still intent on foraging, a task well-suited to searching far for dry hardwood. Despite the fact that Mara had not picked their campsite herself, she found no location that struck her as better. The lake stretched a half mile across, its shore alternately high-banked and sandy, with the creek to the west and, based on a dip in the trees, what seemed to be another outlet on the other side. The meadow was high enough to stay dry, flanked with south-facing slopes that rose into steeper hills Mara did not explore. Twice she saw the bears, though always from a distance; she did not see the deer again.

In parts of the forest, the ground grew soggy, and she found a bog not far north, a maze of mud and tussocks in tangles of fallen trees. An upturned stump hung with moss as if it had been draped in tinsel. Mara gathered the moss to cushion their beds in camp; an armful weighed almost nothing. But it was full of tiny beetles, and when she noticed them crawling onto her, she dropped it again. She supposed she could have smoked out the beetles and used the moss anyway, but she didn't feel like it anymore. In the bog's muddy edges she found tracks of the coyotes who chirped and screamed all through dusk and the nights' first hour of darkness. She thought it seemed ripe for wild parsnips and made a mental note to check back.

In the mornings, Mara met Tom in the birch grove for protein bars, encounters whose brevity suited her more than him. When he had a few minutes he reminisced about growing up in the woods, and she listened politely, feigning interest in the peeling birch bark he had made boxes from as a kid, or the tadpoles he'd once raised in an outdoor tank. He pointed out a column of mushrooms growing up a trunk. "Artist's conk," he said. "If you touch the surface, it leaves a mark." He stomped a conk from the tree and drew a heart on its belly with a twig; the heart remained there, crisp and brown, surrounded by the ghosts of his fingerprints. One evening, boldly, he slipped Mara a square of salted chocolate by the lake. The taste lingered on her tongue all night.

Mara had vague plans to fish, and to arrange a line of snares, but those activities took supplies she didn't yet have, so instead she gathered masses of nettles for string and strong tea. In a gully she followed a vine into the dirt and dug up a string of groundnuts, each the size of a small potato. She had never seen groundnuts before, but recognized them from books—a garland of buried tubers, all growing from a single root. Back at camp, she peeled them carefully, and boiled them in the pot until each nut could be stabbed with a sharpened stick. They tasted like dirt, with the texture of old apples. The survivors ate them all and wished for more.

Each time Mara came back to camp, she found water hot and waiting by the outdoor fire, or else mid-boil. Ashley had taken to tending water while the others scavenged, whittled, and built. It was a constant job. For the amount the survivors drank, they needed a fresh pot once or twice an hour. But Ashley embraced the task, posing for cameras on her short walks to the lake, lifting and turning the pot like it was a product in an infomercial. Blowing kisses, flipping her hair. It struck Mara that of the four of them, Ashley was making her own story. Performing without pretension, but not self-effacing, either. She walked the line well. Mara couldn't imagine trying.

When the water was hot, Mara drank it right away. The heat helped mask the taste of algae and the grit of unsettled mud. But secretly she preferred when the water wasn't ready, because then she could sit awhile and wait for the pinprick bubbles to form and rise. She'd prod coals here and there with a stick, as if their arrangement made all the difference. Ashley leaned back on her hands, and Mara would show off what she'd gathered, arranging herbs and roots on the flattened grass, and, one bright day, a crown of flowers for Ashley to wear. The next time Mara came back to camp, Ashley had woven her a basket of reeds. The basket was lopsided and uneven. But from then on, Mara carried it wherever she went, and no longer made a bowl from the hem of her tunic.

Ashley told her she got bored sometimes, boiling the water, so Mara taught her about wild violets. They grew in the meadow, so Ashley didn't have to walk far. The flowers and leaves were edible. You could eat them raw or cooked, and the flavor was mild.

"I know I don't have a ton of experience," Ashley said. "But I want to learn. If you have any feedback, or advice—"

The question surprised Mara. There was one thing she had noticed, but she wasn't sure how to say it. Maybe it sounded like an insult. She decided to try saying it anyway.

"You should be more present," she said. "When you're walking around. You're in the woods, right, but you're not walking like you're in the woods. Not from what I've seen.

You walk like you're anywhere. But out here, you should walk differently."

"Like, pay more attention?"

Mara had never tried to describe this before, or even thought about it much, and she struggled for words.

"It's almost like you have to pay less attention. At least to any one thing. Relaxed, but you're just—you're alert, too. You know that feeling when you're driving, and even if you're not looking in the rearview mirror, you know there's a car behind you? Because you're just keeping track of it? It's like that, but for everything around you. You need to know what's happening even when you're not looking. Like your mind is shallower. You can't think too much. You just feel."

That was part of what Mara had always liked about wilderness. The chance to disappear. The feeling of getting a break from her own mind, and living in senses alone.

"I'll work on it," said Ashley. And then she smiled. When she smiled, her eyes softened, like all she saw was Mara.

There was something odd about Ashley, though, that Mara noticed early. Sometimes she was charming, easy, made of light. But she could go dark quickly.

Mara saw it a few times. Once, she came back to camp and found that the pot had boiled over, quenching half the fire. When she went to refill it, she saw Ashley swimming in the lake. A speck in the distance. The cameras waited on shore. She swam for a long time.

When Ashley finally climbed from the water, Kyle looked up from his whittling. "Seems a waste of energy," he remarked.

"Focus on your own fucking energy," said Ashley, and then she froze. "I'm sorry. I don't know where that came from." She glanced at the cameras.

Another time, she snapped at Bullfrog when he touched her shoulder. But most of the time she was bright.

Sometimes now, when Mara came back from foraging, she didn't go to the fire directly. Instead she went to the piles of wood, poured her armloads upon them, and stood there arranging for a bit. Waited, because she knew what was coming. Ashley's voice sounding from the fireside, though Mara stayed focused on her task, pretending for seconds not to hear.

"Mara," Ashley would say. "Come drink. Mara, you gotta hydrate!" Leaning around the shelter with her dark hair swinging.

So Mara went to her and drank. And showed off what she'd gathered—nettles and ramps, wood ear mushrooms, pretty flowers—until together they'd emptied the pot. And after her next walk she went to the woodpiles again, and sorted sticks by their sizes, stomach turning, waiting for Ashley to call her name.

9

When Mara was ten years old, her parents had decided to move from their suburban life in Salem, Oregon, to the country, the broad eastern half of the state. "You'll see," her mom told her. "You're going to have a real childhood. Most kids don't even get to be kids anymore." Her mom had grown up on a farm herself—dairy, in Idaho—and missed the freedom that came with space. She spoke of the country like Mara should miss it too, although Mara had never known it, and so the country had always struck her as a wondrous, inaccessible place.

Still, Mara wasn't sure about moving. She liked school and got good grades; she went twice a week to gymnastics lessons, and was learning a back handspring. After a few lonely years, she had developed a close friendship with another girl in her class. But she had a sense of adventure, and as an only child with few friends, was profoundly attached to her parents. When the family held a garage sale in their front yard,

Mara gamely brought out boxes of toys and clothing, selling her treasures for quarters to the neighbors' children, who had never shown any interest in her at all.

The weekend after Mara finished fifth grade, they drove east for half a day, stopping finally at a patch of dry grass and trees that looked, to Mara, indistinguishable from the grass and trees around it. But the land was theirs, her parents told her, giddy, and their excitement made Mara giddy, too. It had a pond, a rotten dock, a water pump, an outhouse, and potential.

Mara's mom had quit her job at a bank, and her father his job as a builder. "We're only building for ourselves now," he told her, kissing her on the head. He had visions of an earth-bag dome, an eco-home well suited to the dry climate. He'd built one once for an eccentric client and found the process versatile and cheap.

All summer they slept in a tent on a wide foam mattress, with Mara in the middle. Her job was to fill bags with dirt. They were poly bags, each the size of a pillowcase, with the faded logo of a local waste-management company. Mara filled coffee cans with earth and gravel, then poured them into the bags one by one. It took twenty-six cans to fill each bag. When she was done, her dad would tie off the bag, hoist it, and arrange it with the others, which stacked in a ring like bricks. Mara's favorite job was stomping on the stacked bags to flatten them. The bags were heavy, but her parents were strong.

When she was bored, she went to the pond and caught frogs, or collected roly-polies in a box. A neighbor girl came by sometimes. Her name was Stormy, and she was only nine, which seemed then a significant age difference. But she'd grown up on the next forty, and she knew everything about the land. She taught Mara how to peel open honeysuckles and eat the nectar, and where to find fossils of shells in the rocks, though they were hours from the sea. When her dad was out hunting, she showed Mara his bunker, which was hidden under a wooden deck. It looked like plain wood until you lifted a special plank and found a ladder leading into darkness. The girls climbed down, daring each other to touch the dirt floor, pretending not to be scared, and it felt like freedom climbing back to the light.

One day Mara found a snakeskin in the grass. It was a whole skin, almost three feet long, and tied in a loose knot. As if the snake had curled through itself to shed. She thought about showing it off, but the snakeskin felt like hers alone, a secret, and she snuck it into one of the earth bags, nestled between one layer of dirt and the next. A talisman; her own contribution to the build. She told Stormy the next day.

"Snakeskins are bad luck," said Stormy.

"They're not," said Mara. She had learned about snakes in school. How they grew, but their skin didn't, so they shed it like old clothes. Like her family's old life in Salem. She started to explain, but Stormy cut her off.

"I know about snakes," said Stormy. "Duh. It's the skins that are bad luck. My brother touched one last year, and then he got hit by a car."

Mara had met Stormy's brother, and he seemed fine. But she couldn't dismiss the possibility. She went to the bag to dig the snakeskin out, but the bag was gone. She found her father at the dome, pressing barbed wire into the stacked bags to keep them from sliding around.

All the bags looked exactly the same.

"We need to take the wall apart," Mara told him.

"Why's that?"

She explained about the snakeskin, and the bag, and about Stormy's brother.

"Don't worry, Marabelle," her father said. "You trust me, right? I'll tell you what, I think Stormy remembered wrong. The way I heard it, snakeskins are actually good luck."

He was just making that up.

"But her brother was hit by a car," said Mara.

"Is he dead?"

"No."

"See? What did I tell you. Maybe the snakeskin protected him."

Still Mara worried. She begged her father to take the bags apart, but it made no difference. The wall was built. The snakeskin was part of it forever, humming like a curse.

When fall came, Mara didn't go to school. The dome was mostly finished—it had a roof, and a stucco coating to smooth the walls—but most of Mara's lessons were outdoors. She had a waterproof notebook, and her parents told her to write down everything she saw. Birds circling, hawks or vultures. She named the tracks of the animals that snooped the compost pile at night. When she found a flower—clover, say, or a tansy aster—she made notes of its qualities, in detail that increased with practice. In September: how many petals? In November: did the leaves have spine-tipped teeth?

Life in the country wasn't bad. It felt normal, even exciting. Mara slept on a plywood bunk above her parents, and ate meals cross-legged on the ground outside, on a patch of bare dirt they called the porch. They washed clothes in an old bathtub, hauling water from the pump. They burned trash in a barrel. They were always together, the family. The three of them. Mara's parents had wanted more kids, a houseful of children to raise in joy, as they called it. She knew they were still trying, but each season a sibling seemed less likely. They called Mara their little miracle. They called her their perfect gift.

A year passed, and then two. The next summer they built a sweat lodge, and neighbors gathered to sweat out toxins, or play banjo outside and drink. The spring after that, they built a new dock.

Mara couldn't remember when she first felt the change. It had probably been happening so slowly she barely noticed, or maybe it happened after she went to bed, neighbors talking late into the night. It was the way her parents talked about the property. Like it wasn't an adventure anymore, but a life raft. Now they were calculating how far they were from cities. Talking supply chains and solar flares. Mara thought they would live on the land forever—thought that was the whole point—but twice she overheard her mother asking if they should move somewhere else, somewhere even more remote.

Her family always had a shotgun, but now they had a pistol, too, and eventually a gun for each of them. Mara's father made her run laps around the dome, calling for her to go faster, faster, until her lungs stung and her heartbeat crashed in her chest. Then he'd thrust the nine mil into her hands and tell her to shoot. If she didn't hit an old propane tank at twelve yards on the first try, she had to do it again. And again. A person couldn't shoot until they could shoot tired.

"It's an important skill," he told her. And then his voice went gentle. "Even more important for you, Marabelle. Girls need to be able to defend themselves."

They had always preserved food, being so far from town. But now her parents ordered shipments in bulk, and talked about digging a bunker to store it all. They told Mara not to mention their precautions to her friends. She didn't have friends; she just had parents. By then Stormy wore all black and was into Finnish death metal. They didn't hang out anymore.

One weekend her father built a mud pizza oven, and it felt like when they'd first moved to the country. Sitting outside on the dirt porch, eating slices and watching the birds. But then her mother had to ruin it. "This will be good for cooking if we can't get fuel for the generator," she said, and Mara lost her appetite. Talk like that scared her. Scared her that her parents might be right, and scared her even more that they might be wrong.

They had always told her: just because this is our lifestyle doesn't mean it has to be yours. But as Mara got older, she didn't know what else to do. When she was sixteen she got a job at a drive-through burger joint, an hour's bike ride away. She hated it. Everything loud and fast and layered in grease, the people and the shouting. It made her eyes hurt, her mind hurt, by the end of each shift.

One of their neighbors was a mink rancher, and Mara started going there instead, cleaning cages for ten bucks an hour cash. The smell was awful, and it stuck to her clothes. The mink were mean. "Anyone who wants to save the mink," the rancher liked to say, "you know they've never met one. These asshole sons'abitches," rolling his sleeves to show the scars. He was a sad man, and Mara liked him. His wife had died of breast cancer three years before. He baked bread often, and sent her home with warm loaves of sourdough, or called her to the kitchen for a slice, toasted and soaked with butter. Once, sizing her up, he brought her to his wife's closet and told her to pick anything she wanted, that his wife would have liked to see her clothes used. Mara picked a thick sweater, hand-knit with a pattern that looked like eagles. She wore the sweater the next time she came by, thinking it might please him. But it seemed to make him sadder. After that, the rancher didn't invite her in as much. She still cleaned the cages, but now he left money under a rock outside.

When Mara had saved enough, she bought an old station wagon. She put blankets in the back and went for longer and longer drives. Days at a time. Then a week, two. She hoped she'd know where she was going when she got there, but she never did.

In Mukilteo, on a bulletin board outside a food co-op, she saw an ad for a survival school seeking instructors. It seemed as good a job as any, and easier than most. Mara called from a pay phone and was invited to come by in three days for an interview.

Eighteen people showed up to the interview. It was a group test. The applicants had four hours to start a fire, build a shelter, and acquire some kind of food. The weather was drizzling, and half the applicants dropped out in the first hour. They said it was too hard to start a fire in the rain. One of them called it impossible. The statement fascinated Mara; she had never seen someone be so confidently wrong.

By afternoon, Mara had a good flame in the opening of a debris hut, and all her clothes were dry. When Bjørn stopped by, she offered him grilled fish on a skewer. She started work two days later.

From that first week, Mara was partnered with Ethan, who had worked at Primal Instinct for a year. She slept in her car and showered at truck stops. She liked the work, which was better than other work she'd done, and she liked that she was good at it. She liked Ethan enough, too. He was a lapsed Catholic and he played guitar. After a month of dating, he asked her to move in with him, and she did.

For a while Mara drove home twice a month. But it seemed that each time she saw her parents, there was something new they were worried about, something she felt a burden to fix, though she could not. They recounted terrible things with the awe of discovery. That her mother's miscarriages were caused by chemicals in commercial corn, a conspiracy to keep the population in check. "It all makes sense," Mara's mother told her. "You know how hard we tried." There were plots by elites to manipulate science, to brainwash, to poison and sedate. It was dangerous, her mother said, to know these things. It made them a target.

"Aren't you worried?" Mara asked her dad. While her mother ranted, she watched him, wishing he would wink to her, signal it was all a joke. But instead he stopped answering the phone when Mara called, noting that it might be tapped, and eventually he got rid of his phone completely.

Someone was always watching, Mara's parents warned her. Always trying to overhear. Mara stopped coming home as much, and spent her days with Ethan, who was earnest and rarely afraid. He taught her French, which he had studied at Reed, and she taught him to fish. Life wasn't good, but it was better. It was better to be away.

There was a strange way, for Mara, that being on the show was a relief. She didn't have to consider the surreality of dark figures spying, or cameras in the trees. There was nothing to research, to doubt or to believe. The cameras were real, and everyone knew it. The eyes were always there.

10

Ashley was hungry. They all were. Mara had never eaten so little, and it made more of a difference than she cared to admit. By the eighth day, she saw it in her teammates: how they paused after standing, hesitating before each step. Hands on tree trunks as they walked, reaching for stability. The shelter sounded with growling stomachs, the white noise of their days and nights. Mara hoped for more groundnuts, the size and starch of them, but though she searched again in drainages and the bog, she couldn't find any more. Instead she gathered nettles and ramps for their daily water-and-greens stew, and though the survivors ate dutifully, the stew did little to salve their hunger and was, frankly, not even good. The ramps soured their breath and their stomachs; the smell of onion seemed to seep from their pores.

When Mara's mind wandered, it went to food. Pasta in cheese sauce, or burgers on the grill. After the meals she'd eaten as a child, foraged veggies and wild meat, she thought she had an appreciation for food. The work it required, and the gratitude a full belly deserved. But there was a difference between appreciating and understanding. A difference between knowing what you have and knowing what it's like to live without it.

The year after Mara's family moved east, their lab had puppies. She was a fat old dog, or at least they thought she was fat and old when she showed up one day and never left. But that was just her way of being. Slow and careful, calmer than her age deserved. They put her on a diet, but she kept growing. Thin in the spine and round in the belly. The fur fell from her stomach in tufts, and one day she started digging. She'd dig a trench, lie down inside it, and then change her mind and dig another one somewhere else. In the morning she had nine squeaking pups.

Mara was obsessed with them. All day long she sat by the squirming pile, first touching the pups with one finger, then picking them up and pressing them to her cheek. How each one fit in a single palm. How soft and slippery their fur. The puppies seemed impossibly small, like they were hardly alive. Not like dogs. Like something simpler, hamsters or mice. Like lost and helpless prey.

Each morning, the pups were bigger than the day before. They grew fat, impossibly fat, bulging and rolling, and the fat in them flattened where they lay, like their bodies were a barely contained liquid. They were everything puppies should be. But what struck Mara about them, more than their tiny paws or their half-moon ears, the sweet stink of their breath, was their desire. She could lift a puppy, and put it down, and wherever she put it, it would immediately lump across the ground in the direction of its mother's nipples.

They could not be distracted. All of existence, the point of existence, was milk.

It seemed embarrassing to want something so much, desperate and unselfconscious. Sometimes Mara felt she should look away.

Later the puppies grew older, and then they were fun. They sucked each other's ears. They found their teeth and learned to use them. Mara's mom said the puppies were becoming, and that that was the pleasure of babies, that you could watch them become themselves. Mara wasn't sure she agreed. She wondered if the rest of the puppies' lives were a distraction from their truest selves, the selves that were made of need.

That was how she felt now, being hungry: that all of life was secondary to need. Hunger was the sun that the survivors orbited. There were other discomforts: rashes, mosquito bites, the swellings left by plucked-off ticks, the air always too dry or too hot or too cold. But nothing else mattered like food.

Each night, Mara dreamed of the bar she would get from Tom in the morning. Even with that luxury, and with the regular supply of wild greens, she wasn't eating more than four hundred calories a day.

It didn't help that Tom seemed increasingly touchy. He complained about the other crew members, whom he deemed unserious, and he obsessed over getting caught. One morning he promised to bring Mara venison sticks, and all that day and night, she imagined the taste. But when she met him in the grove, he gave her a bar instead.

"I thought there might be meat," she said, trying to act like she didn't care. It was vulnerable, the need.

"I decided it would make you too strong," Tom told her. "People might notice." Mara nodded. It was only later, when she thought more about it, that it struck her as a strange thing to say.

Kyle's traps were beautiful, intricate, but they didn't work. He set them around camp, along what he called game trails but Mara suspected were just places water had run in the last rain. He weighted the wooden deadfalls with rocks, and pierced beetles on sharpened twigs for bait. The idea was that critters would crawl under the propped wood, knock the trigger, and get squashed. The problem was that nothing wanted to eat beetles, and also that the ground was soft, so that the one time a creature got pinned, a vole that would hardly be ten calories deep-fried, it simply tunneled its way out. Plus the traps were touchy, so they fell with thuds throughout the day and night, triggered by nothing at all. Each time, Kyle jolted upright, then walked toward the sound with feigned nonchalance, and each time he returned slower, more discouraged than before.

At first Kyle whined as if the animals themselves were at fault for his failure. It took all of Mara's restraint not to point out that the goal of a trap is to catch prey, and the goal of prey is to live, so it is the trap's failure and not the animals' if they don't get caught or don't exist. But on the other hand, Kyle would probably have some philosophical argument as to why that wasn't the case, and then he'd build some weird new trap he'd once gotten a badge for, and she just didn't care enough to have that conversation. Anyway, as the days passed, he got better at hiding his frustration. Maybe he was humbled in a way that served his character. Mara noticed that he fetched supplies now for Bullfrog, and gathered wood from the forest with resigned diligence, even when no one was around to see.

Mara didn't mind him as much, humbled. Still, she knew

that she and Kyle should avoid each other. They got along better that way. Once he'd been going on about his hero, Chris McCandless, and how great Chris would do if he were there, and Mara said, because it seemed obviously flawed to idolize a survivor who hadn't survived, "He's dead," at which point Kyle said, "Yeah, but he really *lived*," and Mara laughed for far too long before she realized it wasn't a joke.

She decided to find meat. Not to show Kyle up—not entirely—but because she was hungry, and Ashley was, too, and she wanted to feed Ashley almost as much as herself. Besides, with their basic tasks completed, it made sense to turn toward the longer-term problems of protein and fat.

Mara's first thought was to make a line of snares. But she could tell by the age of tracks that most of the bigger animals around them had left. Of course they had, with the crashing and voices and smell of people. Any that stayed would be on high alert.

Then she thought of a throwing stick, which she could aim at the geese who sometimes visited the lake. With any luck she could break a wing as they flew, and a goose would fall to the water, and maybe Ashley could swim and get it. Bullfrog had begun to build a split-log shelf for his side of the shelter, which struck Mara as both an impressive feat and a waste of energy, and when he lay down for a nap she borrowed the axe and set off in search of a dense, curved piece of wood. She would have stopped often to catch her breath if her sandals didn't demand slow and careful steps in the first place.

The beech trees had sprouted, seemingly overnight, and the woods were not airy anymore but dense as a jungle; Mara had never seen a season turn so hard so quickly. She pushed through bunches of vibrant leaves, which fell over each other like scales. Even the smallest twigs had bloomed, and the ground rose with ferns that tickled her knees. The familiar sight lines were gone, and she oriented by smaller landmarks she had scarcely given thought to before: a broken stump decked in lines of jelly mushrooms; clusters of trillium, white and blush.

Mara heard footsteps as she walked. She didn't look back. She was used to the cameras now, who followed in case she met the bear again—not to protect her, but to capture the drama. Anyway, she did her best to ignore them. It wasn't until she started chopping a young birch, choking up for control, that she heard her name between thwacks. Sure enough, when Mara looked, it was her.

"You're making something," Ashley said.

Mara nodded.

"What is it?"

"You followed me."

Ashley nodded. "I want to talk to you."

Mara was sitting, though she wasn't sure when she had sat down. Ashley sat beside her. The ground was rough, but she hardly felt it. A camera came closer, and Mara wanted to hide, but maybe Ashley's shine was so bright that no one would notice anyone else.

As if reading Mara's mind, Ashley took her hand and stood, pulling her up, and glared at the camera when it followed. "Give us a ladies' room break," she said. "You know us girls. Gotta pee in groups." The camera backed off.

In the newly lush woods, they did not have to go far to lose the crew.

"Mara," Ashley said once they were alone. "I've been wanting to ask for your help with something."

"Of course."

She took a breath. "You know why I'm here, right?"

Mara knew. To be famous. To succeed.

"Right, yeah. Exactly. I need the show to mean something for me. But I feel like I can see how the story's going. There's Bullfrog building a whole palace, and there's Kyle the scout, and you're gathering plants and feeding us, and all of those things are interesting, you know? And all day long, I'm boiling water."

"Do you want me to boil water?" Mara felt awful. She never knew that Ashley cared, and she blamed herself for not realizing. She should have asked. "I can do it. I don't mind. You can do whatever you want."

"That's the thing," said Ashley. "There's nothing I want to do. There's nothing I know how to do. I mean, I climbed that mountain. At least that was something. But it was just one day."

Mara couldn't tell what she was getting at.

"I'm scared that after all this," Ashley said, "when the show airs, I'll just be in the background. And the guys will get the glory. Like guys always do. It's like that dude, Kyle's hero. He died, and his girlfriend survived, right? But he's the one you hear about."

"You're thinking about someone else," Mara said, but Ashley shook her head to hush her, and she realized it didn't matter, because Ashley was right even if she was wrong.

"So I was thinking," said Ashley. "I was thinking maybe you and I could do our own thing. If you want to. If we came up with our own project together. I know you don't love the cameras, and I don't want to make you uncomfortable, but I think—I think the audience would love it. Girls versus guys.

I'll still boil water," she added quickly. "I'm not trying to get out of that. I just want to do something more. And you're the best one here."

She was still holding Mara's hand. Her voice low, and their faces close together. She thought Mara was the best one here.

"Okay," said Mara. And then, "Yes."

Ashley squealed and hugged her tight. She smelled like woodsmoke. A camera was creeping toward them through the leaves, but Mara didn't care.

"I was thinking a fish trap," said Ashley. "One of those woven baskets. I've seen them on TV, and we have the lake, you know?"

"They're not that great," Mara said.

"Are you sure? How do you know?"

Mara and Ethan had built a basket trap a few summers back. It was perfect—narrow and taut, baited with leeches. They put it in a river full of trout. The water so clear they could sit and watch. But each time a fish swam in, it swam out again. You might get lucky, pull up the trap while a fish was in there, but you couldn't count on your food to stay contained.

"Pretty sure," Mara said. "What about a different kind of trap?"

"For fish?"

Mara thought quickly. "Yeah. A big one."

There was a kind she had seen in pictures, and she tried to explain it. A series of concentric fences underwater, herding fish into smaller and smaller zones along the shallow edge of a lake or sea or stream. It was a massive project; the ones she had seen in photos could feed families, even villages. It would take a long time to build. But once fish swam in, they never got out again. They just stayed. If it worked, if conditions were right, you could have as many fish as you wanted, forever.

Mara had wanted to make a trap like that at home, but Ethan insisted on the basket instead. There was something traditional about basket traps, he said. They were pieces of art. Primitive. You could hang them on your wall when you were done. Besides, fish traps were illegal, so it was important to make something you could hide.

"Sounds perfect," said Ashley. "I'm in. What do we need?"

Mara tried to remember. "About a million sticks to start with. As straight as possible, and maybe four feet long. We'll use those to make the walls. And we need rocks to prop it all in place, and some kind of string to weave it together."

The problem was that string was slow to make, about a foot an hour, and they probably needed a hundred feet in total. At least. But Mara wanted Ashley to feel that she'd been offered a solution, rather than a massive challenge that might not work. The question of string—Mara would solve that problem later. There was no need to mention it yet.

11

J ust like that, they were partners. Mara and Ashley. Ashley and Mara, together.

Most of the sticks on the ground were brittle. So they wandered the woods, looking for trees with the straightest growth. Mara chopped down good branches, and Ashley gathered them in her arms, and when her arms were full they went back by the lake and dropped the load, and when they were tired from walking they sat to process them. Even the nicest branches had twigs and forks they needed to remove. The crew set up a tripod where the women worked, but mostly left them alone.

Shaving the branches straight was a tedious task, but Mara didn't mind. She and Ashley took turns with the knife. Ashley was less dexterous; she angled the knife sharply, and sometimes slipped.

"Slowly," said Mara. "Tilt it more."

"Show me."

So Mara put her hands over Ashley's, and guided them, until they could both cut by feel.

Mara learned more about Ashley those first two days by the lake than she had since they arrived. It was like Ashley relaxed, working together. Or maybe she'd been lonely working alone, and Mara never thought to ask; or maybe Mara had wanted to ask but was nervous, and it was easier to gather plants.

Ashley grew up in central California—not the glamour of LA or the wealth of the Bay Area, but in a modest neighborhood, what she called the armpit of the state. Close to potential, to money, but never there. Her dad left when she was eight. Things got bad, Ashley said, though she didn't specify what happened, and Mara didn't ask. But she smiled when she talked about the pool.

It started for convenience. Ashley's mom needed somewhere to bring her and her sister in the summers, to leave them while she worked at a nursing home, and so each morning she gave them ten dollars and dropped them at the community pool. After the stress of home, it was a balm. The smell of chlorine in the locker room, wet feet on tile. The women around her, chatting and changing, lifting skirts off dry legs, pulling jeans over wet ones. The pool complex was huge. There was a kiddie area, where toddlers in diapers splashed and screamed, and past that a curved, deep pool with cement islands you could climb onto and jump back off again, and beyond it the diving boards and the lap lanes, where the swimmers were serious and fast. Ashley had a favorite cement island, and most of the time it was hers alone, at least until afternoon when other kids poured in from the public day camps. From there she could watch the swimmers, the real swimmers, as long as she wanted. At lunch she bought churros for fifty cents, or corn dogs for a buck fifty, and always waited a dutiful forty minutes before getting back in the water. And as the summers passed, as her sister started tanning instead of playing mermaids, flirting instead of cannonballing, still Ashley watched the swimmers swim.

She was a shy kid. She did not approach them. But one of the swimmers came to her. His name was Jake, and he'd been on the team at Cal. He offered to teach her for free.

Mara wrapped her fist around her microphone, covering it, and lowered her voice. "Was he a creep?"

"What do you mean?"

"A creep. Like, was he into you because you were a little girl."

"He taught me to swim," Ashley said. As if that was the answer.

And so each afternoon, Jake taught her to swim. Showed her how to kick from her hips, pushing the water hard. How to keep her body close to the surface. She liked butterfly best—the explosiveness of it, the precision. Leaving ripples, whirlpools, in her wake.

Soon she lived for swimming. That feeling of power in the water. She found workouts online, strength training, low-sugar foods to eat. Her freshman year of high school, she made varsity. By the next season, she was ranked in the state. And it changed things. Not just the swimming, but being a swimmer. How people saw her; how she started to see herself. It gave her a person to be. Someone important, noticed. And everything was easier when she excelled.

"Like what?"

"Like school, right? My grades got better. But I wasn't doing better work. My teachers just knew who I was, and they liked me."

Ashley saw her sister graduate, start working at the same nursing home as their mom. She didn't want that. Not for herself. But she couldn't swim forever, and though she'd done fine in school, none of the subjects grabbed her. A girl in her neighborhood went on *The Bachelor*, and though she was eliminated early, she made good money after that, getting paid to show up at parties and promote products. That was when Ashley signed up for casting lists, started interviewing for shows. Anything that could keep her important, even in her own small world. Her favorite shows were nature- or adventure-related—she'd always liked moving her body, being outdoors—but she wasn't picky. She tried out for singing shows, for modeling. She auditioned for *Jeopardy!*

"So then you can be famous," Mara said.

"It's the next step."

"To what?"

"I don't know. To getting by."

"But why?"

Ashley shrugged.

"What do you want?" Mara said. "Like, when you picture yourself famous, what are you doing?"

"It sounds weird," Ashley said.

"Look at us," said Mara. "We're wearing matching outfits and starving in some random forest. Nothing is weirder than this."

Ashley laughed. "Okay. You know those nature shows you watch in school? When the science teachers are hungover or whatever, and they don't want to teach?"

Mara couldn't remember. She hadn't had a science teacher in a long time. But she nodded like she did.

"The hosts on those shows, they're always happy. They're excited, talking about trees or dolphins or whatever. Something new every episode. And I always thought that would be the best job. I don't want to work with kids directly. I don't like kids that much. But it seems nice to make a show for them, something they'd look forward to. I'd call it, I don't know—"

"*Ashley's Adventures.*"

Ashley laughed. "I thought of that one!" Then she flopped back on the grass. "It seems like a realistic dream, right? Everyone wants to be a movie star. I'm not trying to do that. I just want my life to be a life, you know? Something that's actually for me."

Mara wondered what it was like to be Ashley. Being on *Civilization*, earning money, was the first big thing Mara had done, and even then the show had found her; she didn't seek it out. But where Mara drifted, Ashley steered. Where would Mara be in a year, if she acted like that? Somewhere better. Somewhere other than here.

They both tired easily. But Mara loved those hours, those days, carving and resting, taking turns with the knife. When Ashley talked, Mara worked, and she felt like she could work forever. Like she dissolved, listening. And then Ashley would sit up, encourage Mara to take a break, and Mara went along with it, because then she could lie back and watch Ashley instead. The furrowed brow in her dry face. Her swift and narrow fingers. Watching her, Mara forgot her hunger. She forgot everything else.

One night, after working on the trap, Ashley woke gasping

from a nightmare. Mara was the only one awake. And Ashley looked around, still panting, and saw Mara in the firelight. She reached out and took Mara's thumb in her hand, and fell back asleep with her hand on Mara's thumb, and Mara lay frozen, and did not sleep at all, and was not even tired when the others woke.

12

They were almost done with the sticks, a mountain of them, and would soon need string to connect them, to weave them into flexible walls they could plant in the shallow edge of the lake. Mara kept telling Ashley not to worry about the string. That she would take care of it. But it was becoming increasingly obvious that without a solution, and soon, she would have led them both on a multiday wild-goose chase with perhaps some of the only energy they had left. The survivors were starving, light-headed, and the trap seemed like it might save them. If only it worked. Mara could feel her teammates' expectation. Bullfrog watching from the clearing. Kyle stopping by with pots of nettle stew, beaming, his hands swelled with welts.

Ashley sensed Mara's stress, but didn't say anything, just nodded when Mara said she had a plan. Mara wondered what would happen if she couldn't make one. If Ashley would forgive her. If what they had together, whatever it was, would be lost.

She tried using the string she had already made, but by the time she knotted a dozen sticks together, she ran out. So she tried connecting them with strips of bark, and soft reeds, and even the thin tendril-like roots from a pink-tinged weed that grew at the edge of the clearing, which struck her as unusually fibrous. But the strands were all too short or brittle to tie tightly, or the knots broke in minutes. She could sense Ashley pretending not to see her struggles, and it was that, more than anything, that made Mara turn to her last idea, the desperate plan she had kept in the back of her mind.

The idea was reckless, and she knew it. If it didn't work, she could be kicked off the show. But if it worked—if she could make it work—then everything would come together at last.

She needed to do it at first light, before the others could interfere—or better yet, the time before light, that first lifting of darkness when shapes swam into view. She'd need every minute she could steal before the crew arrived.

That night Mara barely slept. She was so focused on waking early that she hovered for hours in the space between dreams and the soft, cool floor of the shelter. She heard the mews of a cat, and Kyle mumbling as he flopped to his side. A helicopter lifting and Bullfrog's snores. It pleased her to hear him snoring, because she suspected that he often faked sleep to avoid talking, and this confirmed her hunch. The small satisfaction rooted her, kept her just this side of sleep.

She had taken a camera from a tripod outside. It was small, and surely expensive—waterproof, drop-proof, practically unbreakable. She flipped the screen open and her own green face stared back, chin doubled from the angle. She snapped the screen shut again. Better to watch Ashley twitch in the firelight. Better to do literally anything. She pinched a fat tick from her neck and tossed it into the fire, where it popped.

Eventually the sky became less black. Mara had made it. But she couldn't find the knife.

Normally the blade lived on Bullfrog's shelf, next to some cups he'd carved from burls, so anyone could find it in the darkness. They had decided early on to give the knife a resting place at night. It was their best weapon. If they woke to a curious animal, or something worse, it might be their only shot at defense. Bullfrog and Mara slept nearest the doorway, which was why they chose his shelf. Easy to reach. But now the knife wasn't there.

It wasn't by the fire, either, at least not in the glow that Mara could see. She couldn't make out the shadows. She lifted a burning log by the cool end, carefully, hoping to cast a wider glow, but a spark fell and landed on Kyle's leg. He sat up, gasping.

"What are you doing?" he hissed.

Mara pressed a finger to her lips. Bullfrog snorted, a thick honk that caught in his nose, and Ashley stirred. She was curled tightly with her back to the fire, and she scratched at a cluster of mosquito bites on her thigh. Eventually she fell still. Kyle sat, eyes flicking around the shelter and back to Mara. He was growing wisps of a beard.

"Don't wake them," Mara whispered. "Please."

"What are you doing?"

"I'm looking for the knife."

"Is something wrong?"

"No. I just need it."

"For what?"

"I just need it."

"Why?"

"Because it's a secret."

"You can tell me."

She couldn't, because dawn was coming and she would run out of time. "Kyle. Please. Do you know where it is?"

"I wish you would tell me what you're doing," he said.

"It's a surprise, okay? It's a surprise for Ashley."

Kyle blinked. Then he reached into the darkness behind him, under the shelter eave, and pulled out the knife. He handed it across the fire.

"You hid it?"

"No," he said. "I always put it back before morning."

"It's supposed to be on the shelf."

"I know."

"But it's with you instead."

"I get scared," he said, and the admission was so startling, so uncharacteristically vulnerable, that Mara lost her words. She could not think about it; she took the knife and turned to go.

"Mara."

"Shh. What."

"Don't tell about the knife."

"Fine," she said. "I won't." When she stepped through the doorway, she felt him watch her leave.

Already yellow light pierced the branches, and the rising sun cast stripes through the trees. She made her way on tiptoes to the creek. Somewhere a bird sang, and soon others. The chirp of a sparrow; the trill of a wren. The air was damp. Silver dew covered the ground and the leaves, a crystal shell on each pine needle. A few paths brushed clean of dew, where animals had recently passed.

When Mara reached the creek, she set the camera on a smooth rock and sat down before it. Pressed *record*. A green light shone back at her. "Good morning," she said to the lens. To the world. Practicing. She pictured a million faces staring, and her voice caught.

She cleared her throat, tried to clear her mind. Flipped the screen around. Made sure she was in frame, centered, and that no one could see up her shorts. She hadn't examined her face in daylight in ages. It stared back at her, gaunt and dirty. Her eyebrows had gone dark. She rubbed them with a finger and dirt fell out. Then she wiped a gob of crust from her eye, wondering how long it had been there. Days maybe.

She couldn't let herself get distracted.

Mara thought of other people on television, how they talked to cameras. They had an urgency, an intimacy, and maybe she could approximate it. She tried to sound conspiratorial.

"Good morning," she said again. Raised her eyebrows. Should she wink? No. That was too much. It was all too much.

"Okay," she said. "For the past four days, Ashley and I have been building a fish trap. We have wood, but we need string to hold it all together."

That was no good. Too stiff. She could redo the intro forever. The sun was rising fast, and soon the crew would arrive.

"My partners and I need a steady supply of protein," she said. "A staple food. We're all getting weak. If we have a good fish trap, it could make the difference between starving and thriving. But we need string to hold the trap together. And sometimes, for survival, you have to take a bold step."

That was better. Lenny would like it. He might even forgive her for what came next.

Mara pulled off her tunic and spread it on her lap, feeling goose bumps rise on her arms, her stomach. Aware of how thin her sports bra was. She could smell her own anxious sweat.

The tunic was stained, dark at the hem and speckled with what looked like blood, though she could not remember bleeding. She pressed the knife to the fabric.

By starting at the hem and coiling upward, Mara was able to slice a single ribbon about a half inch wide. As she cut, she glanced often to make sure the camera could still see her. She watched it more than she meant to. Her own body, thin and dirty, on a two-inch screen. Contained. She lifted her chin and pushed the knife harder.

The task took longer than she'd imagined. She needed to keep the knife steady, even as the fabric slid. Cut the strip too wide and it would waste precious fabric; too narrow and it might tear. By the time she reached the armpits, the rising sun warmed her bare back. She cut down one sleeve and then the other.

When she finished, she had a pile of fraying ribbon on her lap. All that remained of the tunic was the reinforced collar. She thought about putting that back on, like a necklace, but it would seem sarcastic, and she supposed it would have been. She plucked a few loose threads from her legs and dropped them on the ground. Hid her mic in the back of her sports bra, tucking in the extra wire.

There were noises now from camp. Voices—the crew. Soon they would come looking for her. She turned off the camera, lifted the mass of brown ribbon, and walked gingerly back.

Tom saw her first, and his eyes widened. But it wasn't until Lenny glanced at her, and did a double take, that the world froze. He was sucking what looked like iced coffee through the straw of a hydration bladder. He opened his mouth and the straw fell out.

"Please," he said. "Tell me I'm not seeing what I think I'm seeing."

She tried to calm him. Thrust the camera into his hands. "It's all on camera, Lenny. I know what this looks like, but it's all right here. I needed string for the trap."

"What the hell did you do?"

"Trust me," she said. "It's all on camera. It'll be good for the show."

Lenny sucked in breath, but Mara felt an odd relief now that the moment had come. Lenny had only one good choice, though he hadn't realized it yet. The show needed continuity. Mara couldn't be shirtless without an explanation. But she had filmed the explanation. She had given him a story. And the solution, the best option, was for Lenny to go along with it. To scold her, take the footage, and move on.

Lenny went away with the camera for a while. Mara heard her own voice, tinny, as he replayed what she had filmed. She sat down and wound the ribbon into a ball. She didn't dare look at Ashley until the matter was settled.

In a few minutes, Lenny came back. He had calmed himself.

"I've reviewed the tape," he said. "And I believe you that this was, ah, an honest misunderstanding."

It wasn't, but that was something Lenny and Mara understood about each other. She would commit to whatever narrative he chose.

"It was," she said. "I feel bad, really. I didn't know it would be a problem."

"You realize this makes things tricky for me."

"I do now. I'm very sorry."

"Yeah, I see that. So I'll tell you what. You can use the string, this one time. But if you push the rules again, for any reason, I can't overlook it, right? Then you're gone. No prize. Nothing. You're out."

Tom, holding a camera, looked up sharply.

"Of course," said Mara. "You won't regret it." But she felt her heart racing. She knew there was a chance she'd be sent home, but she had not considered probation, the possibility of staying on the show in uncertainty. Her old life hanging over her every move.

When Lenny left, when it was over, she turned to Ashley. Ashley had watched from the shelter door the whole time. She pressed one fist to her mouth, hard, and the other hand against it, like she was holding something in.

"I can't believe you did that," she said. "God, Mara—"

Her eyes looked wild, and Mara felt scared in a new way. Until Ashley started to laugh. Laugh until her whole face was red, until she sat and rolled back against the shelter wall, her chest shaking, her cheeks wet with streaming tears. Until Mara started laughing, too, and she couldn't stop, she couldn't stop, she couldn't stop laughing beside her.

13

Mara met Tom in the grove later, as they did most mornings. A few blades of grass nodded and the flap of wings sounded from overhead. But he didn't hand her anything. Just stood and took her in. Hands in his pockets. Mara asked if he had a bar for her. It was the wrong thing to say.

"You know," said Tom, "I'm not your shopping trip. I want to help you, but I'm putting my job on the line. And it doesn't seem like you're taking this very seriously. You're supposed to be surviving."

If I were surviving, she thought, I would shove you down right now and run away with your stuff. Also, now that Lenny had forgiven her for destroying the tunic, she didn't know why Tom would care. She hadn't figured him as a stickler for the rules.

Tom looked at her, and his eyes flicked down to her chest. Then she understood. It wasn't the string that bothered him, her act of rebellion. It was the fact that she was walking around without a shirt.

He sat on a log and patted the space beside him. Mara didn't want to sit. But whatever it was, this power trip, she needed to get through it. She needed Tom on her side, just for one more day. She sat down.

"I was thinking," he said, "that I haven't been fair to you. I kept you from relying on yourself. I made you expect help from other people. I'm sorry about that."

"Please don't say that," she said. "I've been very grateful."

"That's the problem, Mara."

"No, it's not that. I'm not talking about food. I'm talking about—"

"About what?"

"I'm grateful to have you on my side. When I'm here, you know. With so many guys."

She hated pulling that card. But she knew it was something he kept in mind.

Tom's voice hardened. "Did anything happen? If something happened—"

"No, no. Not like that. It's just. I guess I connected with you more. It's been nice to know there's someone respectful who's looking out for me. But I've probably leaned on you too much. I don't want to mess things up for you." Or for me, she thought, now that I have no second chances. "I've been glad to have a man here I can trust."

Tom sighed. He touched his finger to Mara's chin and turned her toward him. Their faces inches apart. She could smell his breath distinctly, the sour scent of turkey and mustard. She couldn't decide if it repulsed her or if she wanted to smell it forever, the promise of food so close, so impossibly far away.

She thought Tom might kiss her. She braced herself. But he only stared into her eyes. He looked sad.

"You can trust me, Mara," he said. "Do you hear me? I'm looking out for you. Even when things get messy. You have to know that."

"I'm really sorry I asked for more food," she said. "That was out of line. And you're right. I shouldn't be expecting things from you. You've already done so much. I'm sorry I put you in that position."

Was she laying it on too thick? No. He loved this.

"You didn't put me in any position," Tom said. "I can see what you're going through. I know you don't always mean what you say. You're a strong lady, Mara. You're still learning, but you're tough."

This was close to working. Close to being over.

"Do you think?" she said. "I don't feel like one."

"I know you are. If you don't believe it yourself, believe me."

He was breathing heavily, and the smell on his breath thickened. Was that tomato, too? It was subtle but there.

Mara felt that the right move was to hug him, so she did. Leaned in and pressed her face to his flannel shoulder. He closed his arm around her and patted her back in a rhythmic, heavy way. "You're going to get through this," he said. "You're tough, Mara. You're an incredible person. It's all going to be okay."

"You think so?"

"Mara, of course. You're amazing."

Mara felt suddenly that she might cry. But that didn't make sense. She knew that the reason her eyes stung wasn't the reason Tom was comforting her. That whatever fear he thought he was speaking to, a different one had emerged. But for the moment, just the moment, she pretended that wasn't true. She took his comfort and made it her own. Turned him into someone else. She leaned against the warm body, felt strong arms holding her together, and took a shuddering breath.

"I know," Tom whispered, stroking her tangled hair. Gently, tracing his fingers on the knots. "I know."

Finally she pulled away. She couldn't meet his eyes. He tucked a hair behind her ear. "You don't have to say anything," he told her, slipping a bar into her hand. "You don't have to say a word."

She clenched the bar in her fist, making sure it was real. It was real; it was there. After Tom left, she hid the bar under a rock for later. Part two of the plan was complete. She wouldn't need him again.

The light cast patterns on the forest, shifting. As Mara stood, she thought she saw a figure in the trees. But it must have been a shadow, because when she looked harder, all she saw were the bright and flickering leaves.

THE TUNIC STRING WORKED PERFECTLY. IN JUST A FEW HOURS, SHE AND ASHLEY wove the trimmed sticks into long, flexible mats. Walls. They propped the mats in place in the water, bolstering them with mud and rocks. Forming a series of pools, heart-shaped, that fed from one to the other, guiding the fish by their curved walls into smaller and smaller enclosures. The largest enclosure was the size of a hot tub; the smallest, closest to shore, was only the size of a sink. The tops of the walls broke the surface of the lake.

Ashley and Mara made a show, for the cameras, of explaining how the trap would work. How the walls curled in such a way that no matter how far a fish followed them, they could only swim deeper into the trap. The sides of the final trap, the smallest pool, were reinforced with thicker wood just in case.

When they finished, the sun had already peaked. The cameras drifted off for their afternoon break. Mara had always assumed the break was for lunch, and spared for the crew a jealous thought, or at least wondered what they ate, imagined the taste of it and the feeling going down. But now she didn't care. She didn't care at all. Soon they would have their own food. The food would come.

They sat by the lake, just the two of them.

The water was settling from the disturbance. The top inches were clear, though muck swirled farther down. A few white lilies gasped at the surface.

"You did it," said Ashley. "I can't believe you pulled it off."

"*We* did. I would never have made it alone."

"We did," said Ashley.

Mara lay back, because she was dizzy, because the sun was warm and soon she would eat. Because she was with Ashley, and content. She thought Ashley might lie beside her, that they could watch the clouds. High and white, drifting fast across the sky.

Instead Ashley turned and lay back in Mara's lap.

Mara's skin went electric, her heart and her lungs. Like the first time she had met Ashley—that sudden shock. She tried to steel herself, to play the feeling off. Trying to act like she hadn't noticed. Like it was nothing, touching skin. She didn't know why she was like this. Why she always had to hide what she wanted, what she felt.

But then Ashley looked up at her, through her lashes, and Mara knew that it wasn't an accident at all.

It was that look. It changed her.

Mara dipped her face to Ashley's neck. She wanted to tell Ashley that she smelled good, but didn't want to make her self-conscious. They had not showered in almost three weeks, and though Ashley still swam sometimes, she rarely ventured far from shore. That smell, though—her skin. Mara's mouth watered. Her mouth often watered now, at the strangest times.

Mara didn't plan what came next. She didn't know what she was doing until she did it.

It was like sinking into a dream, the smell of her. Mara's hand on Ashley's cheek, her collarbone, swirling on her skin. Mara had never felt skin like that. Never felt anything so soft in her life.

Ashley sighed, a breath that filled and emptied her whole chest. Rising and falling. When she exhaled, she melted somehow more deeply into Mara, as close as they could be.

Mara watched her hands move as if they were not her own. Her fingers tracing circles on Ashley's stomach, rising to the cotton of her bra. Sliding beneath it. The way they breathed together, the way they gasped together, the way Ashley melted closer when they finally fell still. And still Mara had not kissed her, or tasted any part of her; and she lowered her lips to Ashley's hair, and kissed her there, gently, and that kiss felt like the most dangerous thing she had done yet.

After a while Ashley turned her face into Mara's neck, and her lashes fluttered.

"Mara," she said.

"Is this okay?"

Ashley moved, and for a terrible instant Mara thought

she shook her head. But she was just stretching, sloppy in her body as she came to. "I just wanted to say it."

"Ashley," said Mara. Trying it out.

It felt like they were waking up. Were there cameras? Mara didn't care. There was no part of her that cared about anything but the body on hers. Not the sharp stones beneath them, the mosquito she flicked from her shoulder as Ashley slid her bra into place. Mara didn't care that they were hungry. That they would sleep in the grass tonight and forever. That the crew had come back and were bustling around, not here but not far away, and may have seen them or may have not. She knew then that she had sensed this coming, that some part of her had been waiting, but she had not believed it, because it is hard when you are hungry to believe you will ever be full.

They made their way to the shelter and lay down there, and Ashley took a nap in Mara's arms.

Still, as the shadows grew long, Mara extricated herself. Pulled herself away. She slipped off toward the creek and found the protein bar under the rock, and then she went to the lake, where they had touched, and sat for a while remembering. Footsteps. She thought they were Ashley. But when she looked up, Tom stood above her.

"That's new," he said.

So the crew had seen her with Ashley. Mara was too high to care. The world would know, and she didn't care. She had never felt this before, the not-caring.

She thought Tom might be angry, and in some part of her mind, absently, dutifully, she lined up the words to reassure him. That he was important; that he was brave, and hers. But the truth was, she didn't need him anymore. She didn't need him at all.

Tom wasn't angry. He only smiled. Shaking his head. Shaking his head.

"You really are naive," he said.

He reached a hand out, as if to touch her, and Mara flinched. He brought his hand back and set it on his hip. It seemed odd that he had approached her so close to camp, but maybe he knew something. Knew that the others weren't around. With the same smile, he turned away.

She waited until his footsteps faded. Until the sun had slipped below the trees. And in the dusk, she pulled the bar from her shorts, the one she'd been saving, and opened it.

The smell was overpowering. Peanuts and chemicals. She imagined the taste, the crystals of sugar and salt, how the first tough bite gave way to a putty that coated the tongue. Surely she could take one bite.

No.

She broke the bar into pieces and threw them in the trap. Plops and splashes. The smallest pieces floated on the surface of the water, and the bigger ones sank, releasing bubbles as they drifted out of sight. Now all they had to do was wait.

There was other bait Mara could use, of course. Insects, grubs. Later, once she had fish, she'd use their guts to catch more, a whole growing cycle. But for now the bar would work best. Human food, processed. Caloric and sweet, like nothing else around. It would take time for the pieces to break apart, for the strange scent to drift out through the water, but it would work. The fish would come. There was no bait like the promise of something new.

14

The next day it rained hard. Lightning flashed through the shelter's doorway and thunder rumbled from all sides. The survivors huddled in the shelter and struggled to keep the fire strong. Raindrops fell through the chimney, and most of the firewood was soaked, but the shelter itself barely leaked. The air thickened with smoke from the stubborn coals and they coughed into their elbows, or turned their heads and coughed at the wall.

At times the flashes came in succession like a strobe light, and Mara's teammates' faces were illuminated and then gone, leaving her blinking, the after-image still stained on her eyelids. She had the strange memory of some black-and-white monster movie, bursts of light that revealed horror for just a millisecond, and as her memory deepened she half expected to see skulls and skeletons flashing at her in place of the others, three beasts by the fire with long fingers and arms. But all she saw were their huddled shapes, so familiar now. Bullfrog hunched with his eyes closed, Ashley's tense brow, and Kyle sitting upright, listening to the thunder intently, as if he might be called upon to answer a question in class. At the next boom, Ashley squeaked, and Mara held her own knees tighter.

The roof held up. Mara hadn't doubted the shelter; she just hadn't seen it tested. Bullfrog had a way of weaving boughs between layers of moss, and she made a mental note to inspect from the outside, once the rain stopped, so she'd know how to do it herself. Curled up tight, nudging and puffing on the coals, she felt like an actor for the first time in days. She knew her role, her lines. Her body was stiff and cold. But her real self was separate, flying, and she could perform like this forever if it meant holding Ashley at the end of the day.

A clap of thunder shook the ground, and they all jumped.

"We should crouch," said Kyle. "Touch the ground as little as possible. That way we're less likely to be electrocuted if we're struck by lightning."

They were already mostly crouching, because the straw was wet, and insects crawled out when it rained.

"At least we're not high up," said Ashley. "Or under something tall."

"There's that tree," said Bullfrog. He meant the maple at the edge of the clearing, the one that was dead and split.

"Good," said Mara. "It'll hit the tree and not us."

"That's not how lightning works," said Kyle.

"I know that. Obviously."

"You actually want to be far away from tall objects."

"Sure, but we're stuck here anyway. Can I say a comforting thing?"

"Not if it puts us in danger."

"I'll take a survey. Hello, teammates. Did any of you change your behavior because of what I said?"

Ashley held in a giggle and Mara felt a flush of pride. She and Kyle weren't fighting, not now at least. This was how they passed the time.

"Fish tomorrow, right?" he said.

Mara nodded. She had suggested leaving the trap for a while before checking it, to ensure the best odds, because even their shadows on the surface could startle fish away from the edges. The longer they waited, the better their chances of triumph from the start.

"Well," said Kyle. "Then I'll tell you what. I'll get us dinner today." And suddenly, in a terrible accent that was perhaps meant to be French, "I hope zat you brought your appetites."

Sometimes Mara wanted to roll her eyes at Kyle, but Bullfrog did it instead, and it felt like he was doing it for both of them. But even Bullfrog fought a smile, his white mustache twitching. It seemed final proof that the world was different now, better, even in the pissing rain.

Another thunderclap sounded. This time it was farther away.

"So what are you going to feed us?" said Mara.

"You'll see." Kyle added another stick to the fire. A lens poked through the doorway, and they all fell quiet. The lens turned from side to side before withdrawing.

For a while they waited, still crouching, until the sky started to brighten. Kyle slipped out the doorway into the gentle rain. Ashley crawled to Mara's quadrant and sat beside her. Bullfrog sighed and lay down, plucking bits of straw from his damp legs. When Mara went out to fill the pot, the air outside felt heavy, like she was pushing through velvet curtains, and she felt the moisture in her lungs. The trunks blackened, the grass and leaves sparkling and dark. Two crows called in unison from the direction of the bog. Everything was warm and still.

An hour later, Kyle returned to the shelter, dripping, with a basket half-full of writhing worms.

Maybe the others were too surprised to object. Or maybe, like Mara, they wanted to see what would happen next. She scooted to the back wall of the shelter, arranging some logs into a backrest, and Ashley followed and rested her head on Mara's clammy neck. Bullfrog stretched his legs and sipped from a cup of nettle tea, which had grown thick and cool. They were a captive audience, but they expected a good show.

Kyle seemed pleased but nervous. For all his talk, it was rare that he kept his teammates' attention. "I need to use the pot," he said. Tentative. Expecting disagreement.

That was gross, but nobody stopped him.

He lifted the worms one by one and dropped them into cooled, boiled water. Almost immediately, they began to stretch and contract. The worms sank to the bottom, wriggled upward, and sank back down. Dark spots moved the course of their bodies, and waste emerged in brown strands. A constant throbbing process, at once measured and immediate. The worms, when they rested finally at the bottom of the pot, tangled amid grains of waste, were the color of a bruise.

"Is this a Scouts thing?" asked Mara, mildly impressed.

"No," Kyle said. "I read about it. When I'm not scouting, I like to read." He sounded almost defensive. "And see? It pays off."

He fished a worm out with his finger and laid it on a piece of bark, where it pulsed, trying to burrow. Then he pressed the knife to the worm's rubbery middle and pressed down. It fell into two pieces, which each kept squirming. The cut as clean as jelly. Kyle sliced one of the halves in half again and put an inch-long section in his mouth.

For a while he sat there with his lips pursed. If the piece in his mouth was wriggling as much as those on the bark, Mara thought it must feel very weird indeed. She wondered how long before he spit it out.

Kyle squeezed his eyes closed, and swallowed. It was a hard swallow, judging by the way his throat bulged. But after a few seconds, he grinned.

"Actually," he said, "it's not bad. Worms are an excellent source of manganese. So I think we should all have some." Mara had never seen him so perky. As if manganese had been a top concern.

"Okay," she said. "I'll give it a go."

"Really?" he said. "I wouldn't have thought you'd go first."

"Why not?"

"I don't know. You just seem cynical."

"I pick flowers!"

"I know," he said. "It's not really what you do. It's who you are."

Mara had been called cynical and naive over the course of two days, words that seemed like contradictions, which went to show that both of them were wrong. She felt oddly relieved. *Naive* had stung, although she would never admit it. She thought that maybe when Kyle said *cynical*, he meant *sad*. In that case it was sometimes true. She could tell because it wasn't true right now.

The worm felt like rubber and tasted like mucus. Like clearing a wad of phlegm from your throat, but if the phlegm had textured segments, and skin. A burst at the end, sour like vinegar, with a hint of a bitter kick. It was not a monstrous sensory experience, but still unpleasant, although Mara had eaten horrible things before and surely would again.

The trick was to stop yourself from thinking. To let your mouth and your throat take over, to chew and swallow like they already knew how to do. Or better yet, to swallow whole. When Mara was done, she ate a second piece, just to show off. Kyle beamed.

"My turn," said Ashley, sitting up. She lifted a piece of worm in the air, above her face, and squinted as if peering through a glass. Pinkie out. Then she swallowed it. She blew a kiss to the camera in the doorway—Mara had not noticed it was back—and laughed. Mara realized she had held her breath since the moment Ashley sat up.

They all turned to Bullfrog.

"I don't even eat vegetables at home," he said.

"You're not at home," said Mara.

"It's not a vegetable," said Ashley.

Bullfrog ate a worm.

"That was bad," he said. He ate another one. "Okay," he said. "I'm set for manganese. The rest are all for you."

They lounged and talked through the afternoon, and ate a few more worms, though there were many left over, and eventually Kyle threw the extras out the door one by one. One of the worms hit a camera and stuck to the lens. A crew member had to pick it off with his fingers, hesitant and repulsed, and Mara had rarely seen anything as funny.

She used dried nettles and herbs to make a fresh pot of tea to share. They passed it between them. The herbs were sweet, and the tea was good. Mara had not noticed the sweetness before. Her senses had started to change.

At dusk, Ashley nudged her. "Can we check the trap now?"

"No," Mara said. "We should do it in the morning. Then we can do it in daylight. You should be the one to check." She knew Ashley would like that. "Besides, the fish are more likely to swim in at night."

It came easily, the lie, and Mara hardly noticed until she had already told it. The truth was that she didn't want to move. And what if there were no fish in the trap yet? She wanted to make sure that the first time they checked, it was successful. And anyway, right now they were happy. They didn't need fish right now.

The strange thing about hunger was that after waiting for so long, it didn't seem like a big deal to wait a little more. What was one more night with empty stomachs? Mara didn't want to leave the shelter, with Ashley warm against her skin. She didn't want to break the day.

15

Mara slept heavy, heavier than since she had first arrived, and woke to her name, to Ashley's voice.

"Mara." Shaking her shoulder. Had she and Ashley spooned all night? Kyle and Bullfrog were still asleep, and the fire had sunk low, but there was new wood on the glowing coals. Ashley had been up to tend it. She was getting better with fire.

It was the kind of gray morning that would burn clear by noon, with mist on the lake, white and swirling. Ashley took Mara's hand, and Mara let her lead. She knew where they were going. But she would have let Ashley lead her anywhere. They scrambled down the bank to the lakeshore.

In the trap were two perch.

Swishing their tails, almost dreamy. As if they did not know they were trapped, or if they did, they didn't mind; as if they lived there now. Waiting to be found. One perch was about seven inches long, and the other quite large, maybe ten or eleven inches. Mara noticed a few crumbs from the protein bar sunk to the bottom mud, but they were subtle. She didn't think anyone else would notice.

"Do you know what they are?" Ashley said.

"They're perch," said Mara, and then, as if that wasn't what Ashley had asked, "They're delicious."

Ashley bounced a little in place. "What should we do? Should we wait for the crew? We should, right?"

Mara pictured it, the money shot: Ashley pulling a glistening fish from the water while Kyle and Bullfrog watched in awe. Droplets on her face, and her hair swinging. The climax of an episode, teased before each commercial break. Mara could watch the moment over and over on her phone, online, for the rest of her life.

"Yes," said Ashley. Answering her own question. "We should wait for the crew. They won't get out, right?"

The fish. "No. They're not going anywhere."

"Should I tell the guys?"

"Let's wait."

They sat on the bank, arms around their hairy knees. "My sister made fun of me for coming here," said Ashley. "She told me I wouldn't make it."

"And look at you now."

"It's because of you. I mean, I'd been camping a lot. But in California the whole thing is Leave No Trace. So that's all I did. I could never pick things or build things or, like, start a fire without burning down the state."

"That was probably wise."

"Sure. I guess."

"You're a natural," said Mara. "You're a sport. A lot of people would have gone home a long time ago."

"Like James."

Mara hadn't thought of him in days. "Not like James. I don't know if this was too much for him. I think he just didn't want to be part of it." She thought of the man at Primal Instinct who'd left his camp on her last shift at work. Just walked out. How he'd been content to fail. How miserable, sometimes, were the people who stayed.

But she wasn't miserable. Not now.

"I do this for work, you know," Mara said. It felt funny that she hadn't mentioned her job before. She had told Ashley about growing up on the land, or at least the nice parts of it, but not the life she left most recently. Not work or Ethan. She supposed she was testing what it would feel like to leave them behind.

"Surviving?"

"Sort of. More like helping other people. I teach survival."

Ashley's face froze and softened. Those expressions that passed over her sometimes. Mara wasn't used to them yet.

"By yourself?" Ashley asked. She was normal again.

"With my boyfriend." As soon as Mara said it, she regretted it. But Ashley didn't seem fazed at all. "I'm leaving him," said Mara. "After this. Once I have money."

"That's good."

"You think?"

"It doesn't seem like you love him."

"Why's that?"

"You're here."

Mara wondered if Ashley had someone at home. She wanted to ask, but she couldn't.

For a while they watched the water. It felt like they were filling time until the crew arrived, until they could get to the fish. The mist lifted a little, thinner swirls, and the water's surface was glass smooth. The same gray as the sky. Gnats buzzed around their heads, and somewhere a bullfrog bellowed.

"Do you think I'll look good?" Ashley said. "On-screen. Do you think I'll come across well?"

"You're kidding, right? They couldn't make you look bad if they tried."

"Maybe. You never know how they edit these things. Maybe they'll take my three worst moments and make it look like that's all I am. Or show the times when I'm resting, so it looks like I don't do anything at all. They could make anyone look bad, if they wanted. For the whole world. Even if they promise they won't."

"Who promised?"

"I just mean in general."

"They'd be missing out," said Mara. "The audience wants someone to root for. Who else is it gonna be, out here? They'd be idiots not to make you the star."

Ashley squeezed her hand at the word *star*.

"Seriously," said Mara, leaning into the warmth. "I think you're better than you realize. You're learning fast. You don't complain. Even though it sucks to be out here. That's what nobody realizes, how much it sucks. Everything hurts all the time. But you can't tell on the screen. So if you complain at all, these people on their couches at home get to feel superior, like you're weaker than they are. Or like you're ungrateful for the opportunity, so obviously you don't deserve it. They want to see people crack, and they want to feel good about themselves, because they're stuck at their shitty jobs and we're their entertainment. But they have no idea what it's like. They have no idea what's not shown. Have you thought about that? Let's say the season has eight episodes, and they're each forty minutes long. But they're out here filming us twenty-four seven for six weeks. That's—" Mara tried to calculate in her head, but hunger made her brain slow. "That's like half a percent of our time here that anyone ever sees. One minute out of every two hundred. You know?"

The number was probably wrong. She'd made it up. But Ashley didn't correct her.

"Or," said Mara. "Or!" Now she was on a roll. "Or these people at home, they think the wrong thing sucks. Like they think the problem is bears, when really it's just itching every second for weeks, and never sleeping more than an hour at a time, and never being the right temperature, and having scrapes and bites and holes all over your skin. That's what we see at the survival school every day. People realize it's not worth the discomfort. Everyone complains. We all do. But you don't."

"I'm dizzy," said Ashley. "All the time. And we're barely halfway done."

"You're no dizzier than the rest of us. You're doing great. You really are. And it's going to get easier soon, you'll see. We're all weak right now."

"You're not."

"I am. I just don't show it much."

Mara couldn't tell if Ashley believed her. The mist had faded from the lake, and she worried that Kyle and Bullfrog would come down before they pulled out the fish. She wanted the moment of triumph to be hers and Ashley's alone.

"I'll tell you what," Mara said. "Why don't you get the fish, and I'll film you myself? We shouldn't have to wait for the crew."

"What about you? You should be on film, too."

It was hard for Mara to express how much she didn't care. What she wanted, all she wanted, was for Ashley to feel good. And to know that it was because of her.

"No," said Mara. "Let's have this be your moment."

"Thank you," said Ashley. And she kissed Mara, so lightly that it felt like the brush of a leaf, like a nettle that only stings when you pull your hand away.

16

shley wanted to look pretty. She showed Mara her folding comb, which was buried under a log at the edge of the woods. Told her, giggling, how she'd smuggled it in. She pulled the comb through her long hair, stroke after stroke, but her eyes never left Mara. It felt more intimate than touch. She smoothed her eyebrows with spit, pinched her cheeks for a flush. Tucked a flower behind one ear, casually, as if she'd merely set it there for safekeeping. "What do you think?"

She looked beautiful.

"You look beautiful," said Mara. "Not for being out here. For anywhere."

"It's not too much?" Ashley touched the flower by her ear.

"Not at all. You're perfect."

Mara lifted the camera and watched the screen. Ashley stood in her hands, a figure in pixels. She was more manageable at that size. It turned her into someone you could look at straight-on. When someone's on-screen, you're supposed to watch them. When they're on-screen, you never have to look away.

Mara tried to memorize the feeling of the moment—the chill of damp air on her chest and arms, the buzz of flies, the wet leather of her sandals, her mouth still tingling from Ashley's kiss. So she could remember it, really come back, every time she watched it.

Ashley on-screen, tiny Ashley, tossed her hair and grinned. "Well," she said. "It's time to check the fish trap. Let's see if there's anything there. Follow me."

She slid down the bank and pointed at the water. Mara zoomed in. There were the perch, swishing their tails. Like they'd never moved. Or maybe they were living full fish lives and humans just couldn't tell the difference.

On-screen, tiny Ashley took off her tunic, tucking her mic into her shorts. Keeping her eyes on Mara. On the camera, which was Mara. On the whole world.

She lifted a ring of sticks, which they'd twisted together the other day, and fitted the tunic around it like a net, tying off the neck and sleeves. Mara wasn't sure the net would work, but Ashley caught both fish in a single scoop. They thrashed in the fabric, gleaming scales, and droplets landed on the lens.

"Two perch," Ashley announced. "These are some of my favorite fish. They're delicious. Looks like it's time to wake the boys for breakfast." Then she changed. She took a breath so deep it seemed to rise into her face, and swallowed, and then she squealed. "Mara, we did it! Oh my god. This is real. Mara. You can stop filming now. We did it!"

She flew into Mara's arms, the fish wet and flailing between them, and it was only when Mara let go at last that she saw that the crew had arrived. She didn't know when they had come. She'd never looked up to notice.

Kyle wanted to boil the perch so that no nutrients would be lost. He said they could drink the water afterward for vitamins, and that they should eat the bones if they could. Bullfrog said sure, that might be technically correct, but it sounded disgusting. The fish would taste better grilled, and after worms they all deserved something good. "Not that the worms weren't good," said Bullfrog, and then he corrected himself. "Fuck. No. No, they weren't good. They were terrible."

In the end the men compromised. They would grill the fish above the upside-down pot lid, so that any fat or juices that dripped off would be caught. Mara and Ashley could have weighed in, but neither particularly cared, and Mara found the whole conversation amusing. Pretty much anything would have amused her at that point, short of losing the fish themselves.

Bullfrog fashioned a grate of woven sticks and balanced it on the pot lid, which he placed on a mound of hot coals. The fish he gutted and cut into chunks, scales and heads and all. Their flesh was translucent, almost pearly, but as it cooked it turned white. It smelled mild and sweet. The survivors broke the chunks apart and ate their first bites together.

The taste was more than delicious; it was ecstatic. Thick, oily flakes breaking in Mara's mouth. Tender and rich and overwhelming. She had the strange and distinct feeling that she could taste it with her whole body. The energy from the fish flowing from her mouth into her blood, into her arms and legs, strengthening them by the second. An actual tingling in her limbs, as her muscles recognized the meat.

Mara ate more. She wished they had salt. Or breading and

tartar sauce, a squeeze of lemon, fried potatoes in a greasy mound. She pictured the whole feast, and then the image faded, and there were chunks of fish on squares of bark, fish flaking, filling her mouth, sliding down her throat. For the first time in weeks, the survivors could eat their fill.

Within a few bites, Mara was no longer hungry. A few bites after that she felt stuffed and exhausted, as if a heavy weight pulled her eyelids down. But she kept eating, kept chewing, and she could tell by the others' sudden lethargy that they were doing the same. Forcing the fuel in. As much as they could take.

Later, looking back, Mara couldn't recall if the crew acted strange that day, or if it was only in retrospect that she interrogated their behavior. There were just three camera guys, Tom and two others, standing around. Didn't there used to be more? A blond one? The survivors ate fish around the fire outside, and the crew and their cameras watched in silence and left at intervals to conference in the trees. That seemed normal enough, although maybe they conferenced more often than usual, or for longer periods of time. She didn't know. Maybe the survivors' meal was boring to film, eventually. A shift from bliss to diligent chewing, and the bubbling sound of stomachs unused to being full.

At one point she looked up and noticed that Lenny wasn't there, and recalled that she hadn't seen him all day, or even the day before. Was that strange behavior? Out of character? Maybe the strange behavior was hers, for even noticing. She rarely paid attention to the crew unless she was trying to avoid them. Mostly she watched Ashley instead.

A few minutes after eating, Mara's stomach turned. Not sickness exactly, but she rushed to the cover of trees, and didn't make it past the hidden cameras before squatting, emptying herself of contents she didn't know she had. As if her body had clung to all it could for weeks, just in case, and only now could it let go. She glanced at the nearest camera, feeling humiliated and then defiant—if they wanted to see everything, this was what they got. The release came in waves; she wiped herself clean with leaves four times before it was over. Then, finally emptied, she stood back up.

As Mara walked into camp, she spotted Tom waving, gesturing from behind the cameras. He had never beckoned her before. They simply met or didn't. A few times she'd gone to the grove and he never came, and she imagined he must have done the same, although not if she could help it, because she never wanted to miss an opportunity for food. But to gesture here, in sight of other crew members—even then, it struck her as odd. He waved in frantic motions, quick bursts of movement before lowering his hand and glancing around.

He probably realized that he'd hurt her with his comment about naiveté, and now he wanted to apologize. On another day she would have snuck over to meet him, hopeful that he'd make it up to her with a bar. But now her stomach was full, and that made her impervious. She pretended not to see him. She kept walking, facing ahead, even as his gestures grew bolder, almost desperate.

So he would wait, like she had waited. He wasn't the only one with power. Tom needed her, too, didn't he? To make him feel important? And maybe she needed him less than she'd realized. She had fish now, and more fish coming. She had Ashley.

In retrospect, she would consider that moment a million times. What was Tom so desperate to tell her? Maybe it really was an apology. Maybe a pinch of salt he wanted to drop in her hand, flavor for the fish. Maybe he was feeling particularly insecure and wanted reassurance that his ex-wife didn't deserve him.

Or maybe it was a warning, an explanation, for what would come. For the way their lives were about to change. Maybe Tom had really meant it when he said he wanted to look out for her. Maybe, in his way, he was trying.

But Mara ignored him, and joined her partners at the fire. She never learned what he wanted to tell her. She never saw him again.

17

The survivors didn't think much about it when the crew was late the next morning. The crew came at various times anyway, depending on conditions or factors only they knew. One time Mara had waited for Tom all morning, expecting him to show up promptly as usual. Instead he arrived after the other crew members, still yawning though the sun was high. "We're out of espresso," he said aloud. "I fell back asleep." Ostensibly to his colleagues, but Mara knew the message was meant for her. She crossed her arms over her bare stomach, took a risk. "Gosh," she said, "it must be hard, waking up in your warm bed without espresso." It was a simple tease; she couldn't resist the setup. But the other guys chuckled, and Tom flushed a deep red.

Mara regretted the comment immediately. She needed Tom as an ally, and she'd forgotten how easily men were shamed. But he met her later and brought up the tension himself, before she could say a word. "No espresso, huh," he said, blushing again. "You really got me."

"It was a joke," she said. "Obviously you can sleep in if you want."

"I know that," he said. "Obviously." But he never mentioned espresso again.

So when Tom didn't show up that morning, Mara's first thought was that she had offended him, pushed him too far. And though she was still high on the taste of fish, and on Ashley's affection, she had come down enough to understand that she could use Tom, or might conceivably need him again over the next weeks. She was in no position to throw allies away. Plus she'd grown hungry again overnight, and she wanted her daily bar. There was something comforting about consuming a substance so obviously man-made.

So Mara felt relieved when the rest of the crew didn't come, either, even as the sun rose high. She had not burned a bridge that, however frustrating, still had a chance of getting her somewhere.

In fact, the mood in camp that morning was one of having been granted reprieve, an unexpected vacation. They found three more fish in the trap, two small but one quite significant—it had whiskers; Bullfrog called it a lawyer—and cooked and ate them and lazed in the grass. Then Mara worked on weaving an open basket that might serve as a fish scoop, or net, and that wouldn't require wetting a tunic. When the sun grew stronger, she spread ashes on her skin. Ashley massaged them into Mara's shoulders, gently on the parts that had burned and peeled, and more deeply on the small of her back, which had only tanned.

The survivors seemed, without discussion, to have agreed

upon a rest day, and it was not unfathomable that the crew might have come to the same conclusion. Probably they were editing footage in their own camp. Or eating croissants. Whatever it was crews did. As the day wore on, Mara began to feel hopeful that they wouldn't show up at all, and that she would get to go a whole day without the painstaking performance, the self-conscious conversations, the creaks of twigs and footsteps that followed wherever they walked. As much as Mara hated to admit she cared, she felt pressure to be interesting around the cameras, and had the crew been present she might have felt, if not guilty, a little awkward about taking the afternoon to do nothing at all. Of course there were still cameras in the trees. But at least they were static, part of the scenery.

Sure enough, nobody came, and they were free.

Ashley seemed a little anxious, but Mara distracted her with food. They ate fish and dumped the guts and bones back into the trap, and then they drank hot broth from the drippings. The broth was rich and filling in its own right.

By afternoon there was a whole new perch in the trap, just waiting. It was beginning to seem, however inconceivable, that they would simply find fish there each time they checked. Like opening the door of the refrigerator. If it kept going like this, Mara thought she might make another large basket to submerge at the edge of the water, or maybe dig a seep well—somewhere to store the fish alive if they could not eat them as fast as they came. Then Ashley kissed her, sweet small kisses, and they gave each other compliments in the shade. That day felt like a gift, like a full-belly laze of possibility. It was the last gift they got for a long time.

18

Lenny had never pretended to be above tricks if he thought they'd make good television. So when the crew didn't show up the next day, Bullfrog decided that this was an intentional strategy on their part. It had to be a plan to see how the survivors acted when they were alone, so the audience could watch them in something closer to a natural environment. Mara picked some more sumac shoots, which were on the verge of tough, but would be edible if she boiled them. Then, feeling strong, she walked around the bog, gathering chanterelles and nettles on the way. The trees creaked around her. Something burst from the ground, a flurry of wings, and she jumped. It was only a grouse.

Back at camp, the survivors munched on boiled sumac while discussing their options. Kyle had a theory he was hopeful about. He suggested that there had been an accident, and the crew was gone forever.

"That's not actually good," said Mara. "That's not something we want."

"Of course it is," said Kyle. "That's why we're all here, right? To test our survival skills. There's nobody better prepared than we are. We'll be legends."

"It could be a holiday," said Ashley. "Memorial Day."

Kyle checked his carved calendar, counted on his fingers. "Nope," he said. "That was last week."

"Or they needed to get supplies or something," said Ashley.

Bullfrog spit a wad of phlegm on the grass.

"Maybe it's a twist," said Kyle. "Like, the first part of the show was figuring out if we can survive here, and we did that. We built a nice shelter and we acquired a reliable source of food." Mara noticed his use of the word *we* for both shelter and fish, neither of which he'd been instrumental in, but Kyle was so hopeful and harmless that she just caught eyes with Bullfrog and let him carry on.

"We succeeded," continued Kyle. "We won the first part of the challenge. And the second part is seeing how long it takes us to realize that we have to get out. And then we'll navigate the terrain, launch an expedition to get ourselves back home—"

"What about our prizes?" said Mara. "I'm not going anywhere without money."

"Didn't the contract say we'd get paid when we complete the challenge? Maybe that really means getting out. They just phrased it so we'd assume it meant, like, staying in the same place for a month and a half." Now Kyle was on a roll. "Plus, think of the name even. *Civilization*. What if we're not the civilization in question? What if it's about finding our way back to civilization? It's genius. I can't believe no one's done this before. So we just have to, I don't know, smoke a lot of fish, so we have food for the journey. And then pick a direction and walk our way out."

"There isn't," said Ashley.

It was the first time she'd spoken, and they all turned to her. She sat stiffly; there was something odd in the way she held her shoulders. "There's no way out," she said. "I climbed that mountain, remember? We could see in every direction. Every horizon. There were no lights, no roads. Nothing at all. Just trees and lakes as far as you could see."

"The helicopter ride," said Kyle. "It was what, forty minutes? That puts us a hundred miles from a road."

"Sure," said Bullfrog. "If we flew in a straight line. And if we pick the right direction. A hundred miles from a road, somewhere in the northwoods. Really narrows it down."

Kyle turned back to Ashley. "You must have missed something on the mountain. Maybe that's why Lenny wanted you up there in the first place. So one of us would have an idea about where to go."

"I was looking," she said. "I know."

For the first time, Mara felt worried. She saw Ashley's discomfort and wanted to shield her from it, to take that emotion away and replace it with whatever it was they'd been swimming in for days. She felt angry at the crew for messing things up, when everything had been going great. She put her arm around Ashley's shoulders.

"So then rescue," said Kyle. "The challenge isn't about getting out. It's about signaling someone to come here."

"We've had a fire going for weeks," said Mara. Short of a few commercial airliners, specks in the sky, no one had passed their way.

"That means we need something bigger. Something huge. A bonfire. Or an SOS sign. Morse code." Kyle was practically vibrating, like he'd been waiting for this moment his whole life. "That's the thing about this experience," he said. "It's not as good as real survival, but it's something, you know? Most people don't do anything this big in their whole lives. And you know everyone will watch it." Still talking, he stood up, steadied himself in the doorway of the shelter, and set off for some purpose only he knew.

Bullfrog watched Kyle go. "Let's see what the kid comes up with," he said. Then he left, too.

Mara turned to Ashley, whose face was pressed to her knees. "It's gonna be fine. This is just the game. And hey, we're together, right?"

Ashley didn't smile. She didn't remind Mara that they had fish, an amount of fish that would have been inconceivable just three days ago, and that food would make everything easier. She didn't put her forehead to Mara's shoulder, or squeeze her dirty hand. She didn't even lift her head for a while. And when she did, she didn't look at Mara at all.

Instead she stood up, walked to the lake, dropped her mic on the shore, and waded out in her clothes. She swam to the deepest water. She swam for a long time.

WHEN MARA HEARD FOOTSTEPS SHE THOUGHT IT WAS CREW, AND FELT A SURGE OF relief, more even than she expected. How caught up she'd gotten in the others' worries, their theories. Of course things were still simple. That was the promise of *Civilization*, wasn't it? That they could come here and just live, just survive.

But the footsteps were Bullfrog. He carried a cardboard

box in both arms. Mara could tell, from a distance, that the box was breaking; he hoisted it twice with his thigh. Then he put it down by the fire.

"I found their camp," he said.

He didn't need to say it was unoccupied.

He pulled things from the box one by one. There were ramen cups, a stained hoodie, a wind-up flashlight, two glow sticks, a deck of cards, a first aid kit, and three boxes of Girl Scout cookies. There was also a box of the same bars that Tom had given Mara, and for some reason that bothered her: that the bars weren't something he'd packed himself, from his own supply, or even that he thought she'd like, but just company property he'd grabbed along the way.

"Maybe we shouldn't," said Mara. "I can't break any more rules."

"Fuck it," said Bullfrog. "You're not breaking anything. Rules are, we use what we find."

He handed Mara the hoodie, and she put it on. On second thought, she slid her arms into the torso and removed her sports bra, pulling it out the neck. She hadn't taken the bra off since her arrival, had even bathed in it in the stream, and the fabric was oily, stained with sweat. It was bliss to take it off.

The hoodie fabric was synthetic, silky in an artificial way, and cool, though it warmed quickly. She felt guilty, wearing it. As if Lenny would appear from behind a tree, or was watching the cameras that very moment.

Ashley and Kyle appeared in the doorway.

"Oh my god," said Ashley. "Girl Scout cookies."

"We sold popcorn," said Kyle, but everyone ignored him.

They agreed to split the cookies evenly. The boxes had two tubes, which made six. The survivors each got their own tube and put two aside for later. The cookies were mint chocolate, crisp and pristine. Mara put a whole cookie in her mouth and crunched down. A rush of warmth passed through her.

Bullfrog explained. He had set off in the direction the crew came from each morning, the direction they left in each night. There was a wide track of bent grass and scuffed dirt, and he followed the path to a camp about a mile away. Two wall tents, canvas, easy to spot from a distance. One held cots, which were bare; the other held supplies. Most of the supplies were electronics, but there was food, too, and a few other miscellaneous things. Bullfrog had gathered the items that seemed most useful, and he planned to go back for more. Mara thought it was strange that the crew had left food out in bear country.

"It's all part of the plan," said Kyle. "Of course they left stuff for us to find. They're clues. They mean something."

"Mean what?" Mara regarded the supplies, which they'd spread on the dirt before the fire. The cheap flashlight. Ramen. They didn't seem like clues. They seemed like scraps, or treasure.

"Well, I don't know yet," said Kyle. "The whole point is that we have to figure it out."

The ramen was spicy chicken. The flashlight was some cheap store brand. The hoodie said *Florida Gators* on one sleeve.

"According to these clues," said Mara, "we have to catch an alligator with a flashlight and season it with MSG."

"It's not funny," said Ashley.

"I'm sorry," said Mara. "You're right. It's not."

"We need to solve a crime with a chicken from Florida," said Bullfrog.

"Please stop," said Ashley.

Mara took her hand.

"It's okay," Mara told her. "I didn't mean to joke. I'm just not worried. Do you know how much trouble the show would be in if they left us here?"

"A lot."

"Right. So much. They'd be fucked forever. They'll be back. And if not, then Kyle's onto something. It'll work out."

Ashley seemed reassured, and Mara kept talking, whispering comforts, as Kyle arranged the treasures and Bullfrog lay down to pretend to nap. Mara said everything she could think of to soothe Ashley, to keep her happy and content. Telling her that of course they were still on television, that this was all part of the game. There were clues, obvious clues, and they would solve them. But she wasn't sure she believed it.

Because Mara had noticed something odd when she went to the trees to pee. The cameras around them had gone out—no blinking green lights, the kind that flashed so quick you thought you'd imagined it. The batteries had died, and no one had replaced them. The survivors weren't on camera anymore.

19

Nobody mentioned the dead cameras, so Mara sure wasn't going to bring it up. But she put aside the rest of her tube of cookies, and went to the lake for more fish. The trap held another perch and a walleye. The others made ramen in the pot, but Mara insisted on adding fish to it, too. "We should show that we're still survivors," she said. Nobody argued, but Bullfrog looked at her hard, and she wondered if he had noticed the cameras, too.

She should have been more worried about the missing crew, but she was mostly worried about Ashley. She wondered if she was imagining Ashley's coldness to her. It was hard to put a finger on. Nothing overt. But Ashley let Mara stroke her hand, and that night she slept beside her, legs tucked to her chest.

In the morning they split another pot of ramen with fish, and decided to walk to crew camp. Though no one said it, the survivors wanted to stay together. If this was a game, one of the rules seemed to be that anyone out of sight could disappear.

Besides, they were stronger now, from the food, and strong legs wanted to walk. It was good to have something to do.

Like Bullfrog had reported, the trail was easy to follow. Wide enough for two, though they walked single file. Mara had not explored the woods in this direction, but they were basically the same—a little swampy in parts, low-lying, though the trail traced the highest ground. She saw a bear track in the path and hesitated, wondering if the others had noticed. When no one was looking, she scuffed it away with her foot.

They spotted the wall tents minutes before they reached them, flashes of white through the trunks and leaves. One was small, but still tall enough to stand in. The other was round and large. The small tent held four cots. No pillows or bedding, and nothing else.

There was another lake beside the tents, narrow and long. Tiny waves crawled over its surface.

"They came by float plane," said Mara.

"How do you know?" said Kyle.

"I don't. But it makes sense, right? A perfect landing place. And float planes are pretty quiet. We might not have noticed them from camp, not if they weren't flying overhead."

"What would we hear?" said Ashley. "If there were loud noises here. Would we have heard them from our camp at all?"

"Hard to say," said Mara. "What kind of noise?"

Ashley shrugged.

"HELLO," she yelled.

"No one here," said Bullfrog.

Mara shushed him. She listened. There was a rush of breeze in the trees, leaves swishing together. The slight lap of waves on the pebbled shore. But even these were a kind of silence. There weren't even birds.

"Okay," she said. "Let's yell on the count of three. One, two, three."

They yelled. Bullfrog was the loudest. Ashley covered her ears and closed her eyes to scream. Afterward Mara's ears rang so much that she could hardly hear. But the ringing faded into the same textured silence as before.

"What are you expecting?" said Kyle.

"Nothing," she said. "It was just good to try."

"But who do you think would hear us?"

"I said it was worth a try, okay?"

They went into the round tent. The door was unzipped, and Mara wondered if that was how Bullfrog had found it, or if he'd left it unzipped on his own. It was maybe fifteen feet across, with a peaked roof and a wrinkled tarp floor. The walls were lined with plastic shelves, which mostly held chargers and battery packs. There was a foam cooler with about six inches of lukewarm water and a few floating cans of Diet Coke and Mountain Dew.

The whole place seemed emptied out. The crew members must have had their own sleeping bags, at least. Bags of clothes. A camping stove, or instant meals. An espresso machine. All of it was gone.

Mara cracked open a Mountain Dew and sipped it, once the fizzing slowed. It was too sweet. She took another sip.

"See any Sprite?" said Bullfrog.

She didn't.

"Damn," he said. "I like Sprite."

Ashley found a bottle of vodka. She took a swig before offering it around. Bullfrog brushed it away with one hand. Kyle glanced at Bullfrog, then shook his head. "I'm only nineteen," he said.

"Are you serious?" said Ashley.

But he had already wandered off, and crouched by a bottom shelf. "Look at this."

It was a map, hand-drawn with ink on a sheet of lined paper. A map of the area, ranging from crew camp to the survivors' camp and a bit beyond. Their shelter was marked with an *X*, and a smaller *x* for the outdoor fire. The fish trap was sketched into the water with dotted lines. Other places were marked, too. The bog, and Mara's usual foraging spots, with a skirted stick figure and doodles of plants. Kyle's deadfall traps. A shaded area with the word *firewood* in tiny letters.

Then there were other markings, in pencil, that seemed to have been drawn and erased. Words, maybe—it was hard to tell.

Kyle touched the smudged marks. "Maybe there's something hidden here."

"It's not a clue," said Ashley. "It's how they planned their days. Their assignments. Who would follow us where."

"It could be a clue," he said.

"Not everything is a fucking clue," she said. "Fuck!" And she walked out of the tent, the door flapping behind her.

Now the guys looked at Mara.

"She's your girlfriend," said Bullfrog.

"I know," Mara said, blushing. "I don't know. Maybe she needs space."

"Trouble in paradise?"

"Shut up," she said.

She felt helpless. She took another sip of the awful Mountain Dew, and the bubbles tickled her lips.

"Ashley's just stressed," said Kyle. "She'll be okay. It's a lot to adjust to."

"Thank you," said Mara. "That's nice of you to say."

He nodded. "My dad gets like that. Angry. He always comes around."

"Angry at you?"

"Sometimes."

"That sucks."

"It's okay."

"My parents never got mad at me," Mara said. "They just got weird."

"We should keep looking," said Bullfrog. "Make a plan."

"Do you think I should follow Ashley?"

"No," said Kyle. "It's better if you don't."

They kept looking. Mara found electrolyte salts, a jar of jam, and a box of super-plus tampons. She'd skipped her period from not eating; she put the box back on the shelf. Bullfrog found mosquito repellent and twenty dollars. Kyle found flares wrapped in cardboard on a bottom shelf.

"Aha," he said. "Here we go. This is what we needed."

"Do you think we should sleep here?" Mara said. "I mean, it's a better camp."

"And she's ungrateful," said Bullfrog.

"Nothing against the shelter," said Mara. "It's just that there's cots here. You know what I mean."

"I think we should go home," said Kyle.

And so they did, with full arms. The walk felt longer on the way back. They'd been standing for a long time, and the standing took more out of Mara than she realized. Ashley had come back before them and stoked the fire, boiled a pot of water, and now she floated in the lake in her underwear. The water flashed silver in the sun.

Mara wanted to crawl inside and go to sleep. But now Kyle was pumped and had a plan.

"Listen," said Kyle. At dusk, he announced, he was going to climb the big maple at the edge of the clearing and set off three flares. Three of anything was a universal sign of distress. From that height, the flares would be visible for miles, and anyone nearby would see them and send for help. Then they would all win the show.

Mara didn't like it. It was too easy. If this was a puzzle, which she had little faith it was, then surely the solution would be more complicated. Still, some part of her was grateful. Kyle's certainty offered a sort of quasi solution: a chance to act like they were trapped, and to try to save themselves, without the panic that being trapped would entail. Even if he was playacting, or just playing, it wouldn't hurt to send a signal. It seemed dangerous and a little reckless, but if it was his choice, and his idea, then who was she to stop him? She'd never liked climbing trees.

"Stay close to the trunk," Mara said.

"I know how to climb." But he didn't sound annoyed. More like he was trying to reassure her, and in fact it helped.

At dusk Mara put her bra back on and gave Kyle the hoodie to protect his skin from rough bark. He took off his sandals, tucked three flares in his pocket, and started to climb.

The maple had a thick trunk, as wide at the base as outstretched arms, and limbs jutted out at sharp angles all the way up. Not bad to climb; not as bad as it could be. It was a bit of a jump to the first branch, at Kyle's chest level, but he pulled himself onto it so quickly that Mara hardly saw how he did it, and in a few movements he was ten feet up. Mara started to feel better.

"Watch out for the dead parts," Mara called. "They'll be weak."

"He said he knows how to climb," said Ashley.

She had come back to the others. They stood with Bullfrog and watched, tilting their faces up.

"I know," said Kyle from above. He sounded happy. He clambered onto a new branch, hugging the trunk with one arm, and waved. Then he climbed higher.

The next part was tricky. Kyle had to move sideways to a branch that stuck out from the far side of the tree. There was a good handhold for the move, a knot, but it was out of his reach. He'd have to let go of the trunk and fall sideways, arms poised, then grab the handhold to stop his fall. He was almost twenty feet in the air.

Slowly Kyle turned to face the handhold. He took his hands off the trunk. Now he balanced on just his bare feet. For an instant Mara thought he might change his mind, grab the trunk again, and come back down. But he was readying himself.

"I don't know about this," she said.

"Shut up," said Bullfrog. "Be quiet."

Kyle fell. His upper body swung through the air, and for a sickening moment he held nothing. Then he stretched his arm and caught the handhold. He looked up, gauging the next move.

"I can't watch," Mara said. Nobody answered. She looked at Ashley, but Ashley didn't look back.

Kyle climbed higher. Finally he reached a fork in the trunk, close to the top, and he sat and straddled a bough, wrapping his legs tightly around it. He was small up there. He reached into his pocket for the flares.

The darkness was coming faster now, and it was hard for Mara to see what Kyle was doing, or maybe he was just too far away. He fumbled with something, and his arm jerked. A loud pop. A white flash illuminated him—that thin figure, legs squeezed tight, one foot tucked behind the other. He gazed upward, his face glowing. Mara followed his gaze and saw a red dot arcing into the sky, far above the trees.

The red dot grew into a star, a flaming ball, distant and huge. It trailed a line of white smoke. Kyle was right: the flare was unmissable. When the red flame faded, only the drifting line remained. Even from the ground, Mara could smell gunpowder.

Another movement, another sharp pop. In the light of the second flash, Kyle seemed more relaxed. He leaned back to watch the flare rise. It followed almost the exact path of the one before it. Two cardboard tubes clattered to the ground. The spent flares, dropped. The third one, the last, was the brightest yet.

When it faded, Kyle started climbing down. He was more cautious now. Slower. The moon broke the horizon, and a silver glow mixed with the blue of twilight. He felt with his toes for the branches below him, and lowered himself slowly. When he reached a broad stretch between branches, he hesitated. "Can you guide me?" he called.

"Step to your left," said Bullfrog. "Down. Farther. Farther. A little farther. Keep going." A bare foot stretched for traction still inches out of reach.

"Farther," said Bullfrog.

The toes stretched another fraction of an inch. Kyle was thirty feet in the air.

"I can't watch," Mara said again.

"You see what's happening?" said Ashley. "This is not fucking safe."

"What?" said Mara.

"This is your fault," said Ashley, and ran away.

Mara looked at Bullfrog, who glanced between her and the tree with expressions of equal exhaustion. Kyle could be his problem. Ashley was hers. She headed toward the lake.

But Ashley wasn't at the shore, as Mara had expected. Not in the shelter, either, or by the dying fire outside. Mara found her in the woods, with her head in her hands. Every muscle tense, like she might explode if someone touched her.

Mara didn't know what was wrong. Her heart was racing. Had she been supposed to keep Kyle from climbing? Maybe she should have; after all, the danger was clear. Had she messed up? Was there some chain of events she'd set in place without realizing, something obvious to everyone else?

Mara sat down.

"Ashley," she said. "I don't know what you're talking about. But whatever I did, I'm sorry. I don't want anyone to get hurt."

"You can stop the act," said Ashley. "I know what's going on."

That made one of them.

"There's no act," said Mara. Now she was really scared.

"I fucking covered for you," said Ashley. "I pretended I didn't know. I told Kyle and Bullfrog you were foraging. But Kyle could get really hurt up there. And maybe you don't need anything from this show, but I did. I do. And you're acting like—like my friend, and it's fucking manipulative. And I even thought, Okay, there might be something here. I thought I could be with you, because—I thought I could go with it. But you're using me, too. You're all the same."

What was she talking about?

"I thought you were my friend," Ashley said.

"Of course I'm your friend." Or more, thought Mara. I thought I was more.

"It's not funny. It's not fun."

"What's not funny?"

"Tricking us. You must think we're idiots. I just think the whole scheme is shitty. Leaving us out here like this."

"Yeah," said Mara. "I think it's shitty, too."

"Then stop it. Call it off. I know you're with the crew. I've seen you with them."

Tom.

"You weren't that subtle," Ashley said. "With your secret meetings every day. I figured it wasn't my business. Of course they'd plant one of us, right? To keep things on track. And I got that, I really did. I didn't care. But to let things go this far—it's sick."

The trees were spinning.

"Ashley," said Mara.

Everything was broken. But she saw it now. Of course: If the show planned to leave them alone, if it was all part of a story, they'd find a way to plant a representative. Someone with survival experience, maybe survival teaching experience, who didn't want to be a star in their own right. Someone to guide their partners in the right direction, or the wrong one if need be. It made a kind of sense.

Ashley, Mara thought. Ashley. I'm not on the crew.

He gave me protein bars.

She found her voice. "I'm not. I'm not with them. I wish I could tell you I was, honestly I do. What you saw—it's just stupid. It's fucking stupid."

It was hard to say it aloud, even now, like she might still get in trouble, might still get sent back. Which was better than being trapped, if she was trapped. Or maybe it wasn't. She didn't know what to want anymore. She didn't know anything. And she had promised Tom not to tell, and however irritating he was, a promise meant something. But screw Tom. He had left her there, along with everyone else.

"That assistant," Mara said. "He met with me, yeah. But Lenny didn't know. It wasn't, like, a plot. He gave me protein bars."

"Excuse me?"

Mara explained the whole story. How she'd met Tom in the gravel pit. How he started slipping her food. How she went along with it, flattering him, saying whatever worked. Even how she used a protein bar for fish bait. As Mara talked, Ashley's breathing slowed. Mara couldn't tell if she believed the story. But at least they were together. At least Ashley wasn't yelling anymore.

"You know what's funny?" Ashley said, though her voice held no humor. "My driver, before we got here, you know. She was this young woman. And after she put on my blindfold, and took my phone away, and we were driving, and she knew I couldn't see, she said, 'This is the part where we harvest your organs.' Obviously it was a joke. And I laughed, because what else could I do? But part of me was like, She could be telling the truth. And I wouldn't know the difference. And I would probably react the same way."

"That's an awful joke," said Mara. "If you don't know the person."

Ashley shrugged. "It's kind of funny."

Then Mara had a terrible thought. Worse than the missing crew. Worse than Kyle in the tree. Worse than all of it. And she knew, as she thought it, that it was true. That it was the most dangerous possible truth. And she couldn't believe it took her this long to understand.

"You thought it was good TV," she said. "You fucked me to make good TV."

Ashley didn't answer.

Mara felt herself sinking, collapsing. As if the forest floor was rising up around her. And then it got worse. "What did you mean," she said, "when you said, 'You're all the same'?"

Ashley turned her face away.

"You owe me this," Mara said.

"It's not your business."

"No. Tell me. Who else did you sleep with?"

"It doesn't hurt to get along with the crew," Ashley said. "You would know. You did the same thing."

"Who was it?"

"Lenny."

"Of course it was. Of fucking course."

"It's not like you're single."

"I'm not jealous," said Mara. "That's not the problem. I think it's disgusting."

"Do you hear yourself?"

"Yeah. Yeah, I do. I'm not mad that you fucked Lenny to be a star. I'm mad that you made me part of it." Mara knew it was cruel as she said it. But she couldn't bear the questions in her mind. When Ashley let Mara touch her, that first time by the lake. Was she doing it for Mara? Because she thought Mara was crew, and she wanted to keep the crew happy? Was it for the audience, a performance? Was it for him?

Did she think she had to? When Mara kissed her. Each time that Ashley kissed back. Did she think she had to?

Mara felt nauseous. She couldn't look at Ashley. Was that fair? Maybe Ashley was the one who should look away. Maybe they had both been used. Her throat tightened, and she thought she might vomit, bracing herself while the wave passed. She knew Ashley was breaking beside her, and she didn't care.

Mara broke, too. She started to run. In no direction, in every direction, stumbling through the dark. Something tore at the sole of her foot, and she felt her sandal growing wet, but she didn't slow. Not until she reached the bank of the creek, where she fell to her knees on the stones.

Pounding filled her ears. Like drums, like water. Finally it slowed. Her knees hurt. She liked how the pain kept her there. She pressed her face to the ground.

Here she was, in the kind of world her parents had waited for their whole lives. With a woman who made her feel like she'd never felt. And everything was shattered.

Then she heard the crash and the scream.

20

R elief.

Mara was ashamed to admit it. But her first feeling was relief. Relief that there was anything else in the world strong enough to grab her, to distract her. Something else she could do and be.

By the time she got to the clearing, Bullfrog had cracked a glow stick, and the whole scene was lit yellow. Kyle panting on the ground, one foot twisted beneath him. A patch of raw flesh. Blood gleaming in the moonlight.

I am good in a crisis, thought Mara. I am good.

It was heaven, the way her worries disappeared. The way each second was its own action, and the seconds came in order, like marching soldiers. Ashley showed up behind her. "Boil water," Mara told her, and kept her gaze on Kyle. His eyes seemed unfocused.

"He was almost down," said Bullfrog. "Almost to the ground."

"How'd he land?"

"I'm not sure."

"Kyle," said Mara. "How's your back?"

It took a long time for the words to reach him. Finally they did. "I think it's okay."

She felt down his body, patting his neck and ribs and gut and thighs. Touched his bent foot. It was shiny with blood. "Can you feel this?"

He shook his head.

"Can you wiggle your toes?"

There was no movement, no pulse.

"We should get him back to the shelter. Keep him warm."

Bullfrog nodded. They lifted Kyle between them, and he hopped on his right leg. With each movement, he screamed. He had been thin at the start of the challenge, and now he couldn't have weighed more than 130 pounds. But even with adrenaline and the past days' food, Mara had to stop twice on the short walk to catch her breath. Her ears ringing. Finally they reached the shelter and laid him down on a grass mat.

The walls reflected the light of the fire, the unearthly neon of the glow stick, and she could see better now. Kyle's right leg was scraped from the thigh down, perhaps where he had slid against the trunk. His left foot was twisted, and the skin split like an overripe fruit. Blood dripped down his foot in thick lines.

"Hurts like a bitch, huh?" said Bullfrog.

"Yes," said Kyle. "It does."

There were splinters around the wound. Mara got the first aid kit. It was a white plastic case the size of a paperback book. The kind that were sold ready-made at gas stations and gro-cery stores, and which Mara had always assumed were designed for liability protection more than anything else. See? People could say. Don't blame us; we had a first aid kit. We were prepared.

Inside, the case was divided into tiny sections. There were packets with antihistamines, aspirin, anti-itch gel, and anti-bacterial ointment, though only two of the latter, and they couldn't have held more than a dot each. A roll of gauze, three Band-Aids, tweezers, a syringe, and rubber gloves. If Mara had packed the kit—and she did pack first aid kits, back at Primal Instinct—she would have tossed the Band-Aids and added sutures, trauma dressings, shears, and a scalpel. Maybe some candy, too.

Boiled water appeared. Mara poured it over the break in Kyle's skin, watching pink liquid drain out. She used the syringe to squirt more water into the wound, pushing out dirt and hopefully anything worse. The opening wasn't as big as she had feared, just over an inch across. Mara heard a whirring sound: Bullfrog winding the flashlight. She spotted a fat splinter and picked it out with tweezers. Kyle winced.

"Pour vodka on it?" said Bullfrog, grimacing.

"That's a myth," said Kyle. He sounded short of breath. "It actually damages the tissue."

"I don't know," said Mara. "Maybe out here it would help, though. It's not exactly a sanitary environment."

"Okay," said Kyle.

"Okay?"

"Yeah," he said. "Go ahead."

She tried to remember if she'd ever heard him change his mind.

Bullfrog gave Kyle a stick to bite, and Mara poured vodka on the wound. Kyle screamed through gritted teeth, his face red, veins rising around his eyes. Even his eyelids bulged. As if the scream, silenced, burst from every part of his face. Mara felt nauseous again.

"I hope Lenny's fucking happy now," said Bullfrog.

Lenny. For horrible, blissful moments, Mara had forgotten. And now she heard Ashley's voice from the doorway.

"They're watching," Ashley said. "When they see how bad it is, they'll come. They'll come now."

Mara couldn't look at her.

Kyle was returning to himself. Breathing more deeply. He tried to straighten his leg, then winced and let it go slack. The flesh around his ankle had already started to swell.

"Of course they'll come," he said. "I shot the flares."

"You did great," said Ashley. Her voice cracked.

"I did," he said. "Did you see that part where I had to fall and catch myself?"

"I couldn't watch," said Mara.

"It was cool," said Kyle. "I hope the cameras got it. What were you two on about, anyway?"

Shit, thought Mara. "I'm sorry you heard that."

"Don't apologize, just tell me. I'm injured. I need the distraction."

Ashley didn't answer, so Mara tried to think of a lie. Fuck it. "It was me," she said. "I cheated. One of the crew members gave me protein bars when I met him by the creek."

"You're kidding. This whole time?"

"Every day."

"You've been getting a protein bar every single day?"

"That's what I said."

"I got coffee," said Bullfrog.

Now it was Mara's turn to be astonished. "What?"

"One morning that camera guy, the big one, he took off his backpack and left it by a rock to take a leak. So I snuck out and drank from his thermos. Pretty soon he was leaving it there every day. Not for me exactly, but I figured he knew. He even left a muffin once, next to his bag, and he didn't say anything when he came back and it was gone. Lenny, he'd never allow it. But these crew guys don't give a shit. They're working men. They're here for a paycheck. I think they feel sorry for us."

Mara had never thought about that. Apart from Tom, she hadn't thought much about the crew at all.

"Maybe that guy bet on you," Mara said. "I think they were gambling on us, too. Who would last."

Kyle's eyes were wide, and he kept glancing between them, like he couldn't decide what part of the conversation to circle back to.

"So what you're saying," Kyle said, "is that I'm the best real survivor here. Like legit. Not cheating."

Nobody brought up Ashley, but to be fair, it was kind of obvious. Survival had never been her goal.

"Sure," said Mara.

"Sure," said Bullfrog.

You had to hand it to Kyle. His foot was broken, busted open. He was stuck in the woods with no way out. But he was enjoying this part.

"Say it," he said.

"Jesus Christ," said Bullfrog.

"Say it. Right here in front of everyone."

Bullfrog sighed. "You, Kyle, are the best survivor here."

"I've seen a lot of so-called survivors," Mara said. "I'll give you this."

"Better than me," said Ashley. "Better than these two-faced cheaters." There was a catch in her voice, but not cruelty. Mara couldn't look at her.

"I knew it," said Kyle. "This whole time, I knew it." And when he closed his eyes, he had a smile on his lips.

IN THE MORNING, BULLFROG WENT BACK TO CREW CAMP AND CUT A SQUARE OF canvas from the wall of a tent, which Mara sliced into strips for a bandage. Ashley made herself scarce. Maybe she sensed that Mara couldn't bear to be near her. Mara felt a pulse in her hands at Ashley's voice, something raging, although it wasn't purely anger. She couldn't decide how she felt. Maybe it was pity, or maybe grief. She pushed the feeling down. It was a hot day, and when she went outside, she saw Ashley floating on her back in the lake.

Bullfrog was gone at intervals. Mara figured he was scouting. But he didn't explain, and she didn't ask.

Mostly Mara sat in the shelter and talked to Kyle. It wasn't for the pleasure of conversation. She worried he might have hit his head. She wanted to know if he got confused, or if he started to slur his words. Also because when Kyle stopped talking, he seemed to sink into the pain. Or maybe it was Mara who sank into hers.

"The batteries," Kyle told her.

So he'd noticed the cameras, too. "What about them?"

But instead he pulled out his mic, opened the case. "Can you replace them?"

Mara had taken her own mic off the night before, stashed it in the crotch of a tree. "Sure," she said, trying to sound normal. "Of course."

She tried to remember everything Kyle had mentioned liking in the past few weeks. Scouts, of course, but Mara could think of few things more boring than structured and ritualized adventure. He liked reading, though. So she asked about his favorite books. Mostly history, he said. And then, a little shyly, poetry. Which surprised Mara, although she didn't know why; after all, a nerd was a nerd. But at least it was something they could talk about.

She told Kyle about an interaction she'd had with a student at Primal Instinct, a sure-of-himself type who liked to philosophize at length, and kept signing up for private classes with her, though he spent most of the time saying supposedly deep things and waiting for Mara to act impressed. "There's so little we know about the universe," he told her once, when he was supposed to be tying knots. He put down his rope and plucked a handful of grass at his feet and held it out, shaking dirt from the roots. "We don't even know basic things. Like, what's dirt? What's grass? I think about that sometimes."

"You and Walt Whitman," Mara had said.

This bothered the student. "Who?"

"The poet? 'What is the grass?' He wrote about it."

"You think this Walt guy is smarter than me?"

He'd said it lightly, but Mara could tell he wasn't joking.

"And now," said Kyle, "'it seems to me the beautiful uncut hair of graves.'"

"Is that Whitman?"

"Yeah. That line always stuck with me."

Mara nodded, like she understood, but the truth was that Kyle could have said anything and she would have believed it was Whitman. She didn't know much about him, except that she wrote a paper about the grass poem once, back when her parents were still following an actual homeschool curriculum. She worked hard on the essay, which was something of a poem itself, a list of things she thought that grass might be. One item on the list was *ladders of dreams*, which seemed embarrassing in retrospect, but at the time Mara was proud of the turn of phrase.

Her parents said good job, but didn't mention anything specific. Mara wondered if they had read it. After that, she started putting mistakes in her essays on purpose. Nonsense sentences, and then nonsense paragraphs, even on the first page. Her parents never said a word. Mara was hurt, though her neighbor Stormy was jealous, and told her that anyone should be happy to get out of schoolwork for free.

So when the client mentioned grass, Mara was happy for the chance to bring up Whitman, to prove that she had once learned something other than survival. "It wasn't that I knew it, really," she told Kyle. "It's just that I liked knowing more than he did."

Kyle nodded, like the impulse was unsurprising. Mara had never mentioned it to anyone before.

There was a strange way Kyle seemed happier, now that he was injured. Relaxed. It surprised Mara how easy he was to talk to. She wondered if she hadn't tried before, or if he was the one who changed.

"So," she said. "Chris McCandless. What do you like about him?"

She wasn't sure if this was a good question or a bad one, given the circumstances. But Kyle lit up.

"He became what he wanted," said Kyle. "You know, he threw everything away that was fake. And then he designed the person he wanted to be, and he became that. And he was good at it. Everyone talks about the fact that he died, but they don't pay attention to everything he did first. He's pretty incredible, if you read about him. He built a whole life for himself out in the Alaskan bush. I want to go out to his camp someday and see it. It's still there, you know. People can go if they know how to find it. And it's not really his fault that he died. He ate wild potato seeds, because his guidebook said they were harmless. But they were toxic. They poisoned him, and he didn't know."

People used to debate McCandless's story a lot at Primal Instinct, because clients liked to boast that they'd never make the same mistakes he did. Mara had to bite her tongue. The clients wanted her to be experienced, but in a way that validated their knowledge rather than challenged it, a way that built them up rather than contradicting them. She had learned with reluctance to follow along. Now that she wasn't at work, she could speak freely.

"He didn't get poisoned, though," Mara said. "Someone proved that theory wrong. They think he starved."

"No," said Kyle. "He didn't starve. He was poisoned. It wasn't his fault."

"That just makes a better story, the poison. But really he wasted away." Mara launched into a whole speech about the misunderstanding: how the poison theory offered closure, but really McCandless just went out into the wilderness and got stuck, and couldn't find enough food to survive. It made sense, if you cared about a story, if you cared about a person, to want a dramatic conclusion. But that didn't make the conclusion true. It was still just a fantasy about a guy who died.

Kyle didn't respond.

Immediately Mara regretted her speech. She was talking

about an idea, and Kyle was talking about his hero. It wasn't fair to argue for the sake of arguing when he had stakes in the game and she didn't. She felt pretty bad after that.

She thought about telling Kyle that she'd misremembered, that McCandless must have died from poison after all, but they would both know she was lying. And lying from pity, too, which was worse. An apology wouldn't work, because Kyle would just point out that Mara hadn't done anything wrong. Kyle was logical like that sometimes. It was part of why he annoyed her.

Still, Mara wanted to make it up to him. She couldn't have two teammates mad at her, and this problem seemed easier to solve. She tried to think if there was anything Kyle might really want, something she could give him, but since they shared all their belongings anyway, except for the tubes of cookies, that wouldn't make sense. And frankly, Mara wanted to keep her cookies. So she thought she might make something for him instead.

There were a few things she was good at making, because she dicked around with twigs and plants while waiting for clients at Primal Instinct, and they used to have contests among the staff there. There was one summer when they all made sun hats, and another when they wove sandals out of cattails and got into a competition about who could wear theirs the longest before they fell apart. Mara's lasted the second longest out of all the instructors, which was two weeks. She was pretty sure the winner cheated and used glue. But Kyle didn't need a hat, and sandals would draw attention to the fact that he wasn't walking. That by the look of it, he might not be walking for some time.

A book would be perfect, given Kyle's circumstance, but

obviously impossible. What did Boy Scouts like? Patches? Mara could probably find a pen at the crew camp and a piece of canvas and draw a patch about being on a reality show, or climbing a really big tree. But she didn't want him to think she was making fun of him.

Then she thought of the leather bracelets they gave out after campouts at Primal Instinct. They were tacky but beloved. Kyle wouldn't need to stand up to use one, and they were kind of like a badge, but not in a way that cheapened the ones Kyle had already earned. Mara had never appreciated the bracelets, but maybe they were the kind of thing people liked, if they were people like Kyle. Caring a lot about purity and proving themselves and stuff.

The bracelets looked rustic, like the instructors had made them by hand while waiting for clients to emerge, but the truth was that Bjørn bought them online in bulk. They weren't even rare. If you searched the right words, you'd find them on countless websites. Photographed against pristine white backgrounds. You could buy a pack of ten for eighteen dollars. They came individually wrapped in crinkly plastic bags with cardboard tags. Back at headquarters, when no one was coming by, Mara would go through and unwrap boxes of them at a time. Then she'd hang them in the garage for a week so they didn't smell like plastic anymore.

When Kyle took a nap, Mara went down to the creek, to the bend with the gravel spit, and searched the stones for a while. She wasn't sure what she was looking for. But she found another chunk of quartz, white and glittering and about an inch long, that would make a nice pendant if she could figure out how to hold it. She had a few feet of very fine nettle string that she hadn't used yet, but it was brittle. So she soaked it in water, and after it softened she wrapped it around the center of the crystal a few times to make a wide band, tying it snugly. As the string dried in the sun, it tightened, and when she gave the necklace a few vig rous shakes, the stone didn't budge. It might not stay put if Kyle were big on, say, jogging, but it seemed solid enough for his current state.

Mara was excited to give it to him. But when she got back to the shelter, Kyle was still asleep. His bandage was wet with pus. A fly sat on it, and she shooed it away. She went down to the lake for a while and dug a seep well with a stick, then moved some fish from the trap to the well, and went over to the bog, where she found a huge flush of oyster mushrooms and, to her relief, another long strand of groundnuts. In the clearing, Bullfrog arranged three signal pyres in the shape of a triangle. Ashley was nowhere to be seen.

Kyle was awake now, propped on his elbows and watching the sky through the smoke hole. Mara didn't know what to say, so she just handed him the necklace.

"Here," she said.

"Is this because you feel bad for me?"

"Yes," she said. "But also, you'd be making cool shit if you could. Probably cooler than whatever we're doing. Weaving a couch or something. And you got hurt climbing to help us, so it feels like . . ." She trailed off. Maybe she shouldn't have mentioned the climbing thing. Mara was second-guessing a lot of what she said now, which was new, and she didn't like it. "We're a team," she finished unconvincingly. "So. I made it because we're a team."

Kyle looked closer at the necklace. "Nettle cordage. You soaked it?"

She nodded.

"Smart," he said. He leaned forward for her to tie it behind his neck.

Mara lifted the back of his matted hair and found a patch of light skin beneath it. His skin was rough, half-peeled sunburn over zits that hadn't fully surfaced. It looked painful. She tied a double knot in the cordage and pulled the knot tight.

"I should get more water," Mara said, suddenly uncomfortable. "Before it's dark." As she ducked out, she saw Kyle turning the pendant over and over in his hands.

21

For dinner, Mara peeled the groundnuts and boiled them until they were soft, chopped them with the oyster mushrooms, and cooked them in the pot with the shredded filets of two pike. The stew cooked into a brown mash but tasted like a real meal, meat and potatoes of the northern forest: the starch of the roots and delicacy of the mushrooms, rich and filling from the fish. It pleased her, too, that they had not eaten ramen; with food like this, they could save their stores for another day. If they needed to.

In the middle of the night, Bullfrog tore from the shelter and puked his guts up in the grass. The sounds went on for an hour, for two. Coughing and groaning. Mara brought him water, but he wouldn't drink. The others sat grimly in the firelight, waiting to be sick themselves, but apart from a flop in Mara's stomach at the sound of vomiting, she was fine, and it seemed that Ashley and Kyle were, too. That didn't stop Ashley from casting blame.

"What did you feed us, Mara?" she said.

"Nothing," said Mara. "It's fine. It's stuff we've been eating all along."

"Well, apparently it's not fine."

"I don't see you foraging."

"You also don't see me poisoning us," said Ashley.

"Maybe it was the water," said Kyle. "Maybe he ate something on his own. We don't know what made him sick. It could be anything out here."

"Exactly," said Ashley. "We don't know."

Mara refilled the water and boiled it extra long to be sure. After a while, Bullfrog crawled back in. "I've been thinking I should go for help," he said. "Pick a direction and keep walking. But maybe not today."

"We don't need help," said Ashley. "We need the crew to get their act together."

"Really?" said Mara. "Maybe you should tell us more about the crew, Ashley."

"Do you know something about the crew?" Bullfrog's voice was deep and sudden. "If you know something, say it. Fuck. Every one of us. This is no time for fucking secrets."

Mara waited. But Ashley just shook her head, eyes shining in the darkness.

THE MORNING BROKE WITH AN INTENSITY MARA HAD RARELY SEEN, A THICK AND pressing heat. Bullfrog and Ashley lit the signal pyres in the clearing. They threw in boughs of fresh white pine, which sparked and sent up sheets of flame. The moisture darkened the smoke into black columns.

In the shelter, Mara cut the dressing off of Kyle's wound and saw movement.

It took time to realize what she was seeing. Inching maggots, clustered tight, and the skin around them red. The way Kyle was positioned, he couldn't see it. Mara tried not to make an expression, but he knew.

"It's bad," he said.

"Not that bad."

"Stop it," he said. "Tell me."

"It's just healing."

"Mara."

"I'm serious!"

"Don't do that. Just tell me."

"It's looking inflamed," she said. "And there are maggots."

"Maggots? Really?"

"I'll take them out."

"Don't. I think they help, actually. They eat the dead tissue. It's not like we have something else to try."

Mara gave him an aspirin and a cookie, and he swallowed both. "Try to rest," she said. "I'll be back."

She went to the bog and tried to remember everything she had learned about plant medicine. She recalled bits of knowledge. As a kid, when she skinned her knee or tweaked an ankle, her parents would sit beside her and pull two books from the shelf. One, a medical guide, with which to identify her grievance. She'd flip tissue-thin pages past photos of genital warts and severed limbs to settle on *abrasion* or *laceration* or *sprain*. The second book was a guide to medicinal plants. It was yellowed and brittle. Mara's mom said old plant guides were better, because they were written back when people actually used the knowledge.

When she cut herself with her pocketknife, for instance—a laceration—Mara had to find yarrow. *Millefolium, million leaves,* named for the leaflets that clustered almost as densely as the white buds above them. Its traditional name offered a clue: Soldier's Woundwort. A blood stopper. She knew where it grew, in the ditch between the mailbox and the road, right at the edge of the property. She'd chew the leaves into a paste, the sharp herbal taste of them, and apply the paste to the cut until it stopped bleeding. It felt like she had really done something, some ancient practice, although probably the bleeding would have stopped by then on its own.

Her mom always said that plants helped the body heal. That there was chemistry in plants that humans would never understand, and couldn't approximate in a lab. Ancient chemistry, if you knew how to use it. Unlike modern medicine, she said, which isolated one substance and pumped you with it until you got better or died, or just as likely stayed sick forever. Mara's mom believed that modern people were sick in ways they didn't realize, every one of them walking off-balance, a balance that could only be fixed with nature, with the remedy of plants and time.

She wasn't even against doctors. Neither of Mara's parents were. They still brought her to the pediatrician, the dentist. She took antibiotics for strep throat, and got a tetanus shot when she scraped her knee on a rusty nail while jumping the fence from a cow pasture two miles away. Back then, at least, her parents didn't deny the merits of modern life; they just liked a simpler world better, or the idea of a simpler world. Plant medicine and mutual aid. Community, they said, was the best resource a person could have, as long as your community shared your values. Mara wondered if Kyle and Bullfrog and Ashley shared her values. She wondered if her parents went to the doctor anymore.

Mara remembered some of the medicinal plants, of course. Plantain for stings and rashes, willow bark for fever, horsemint for toothaches, elderberry for colds. But she hadn't seen them all here. The vegetation was different, the climate drier and colder. And there was no plant that would fix Kyle's leg. They needed a doctor for that.

But maybe there was something to slow infection, if not treat it. Buy them the time they needed. Echinacea helped the immune system, but did that count for wounds? Mara hadn't seen any. Ginseng had similar properties, and might grow around here. Balsam fir—what did balsam fir do again? Mara found a fir tree and broke off the tips with the freshest growth and gathered them in her basket. She couldn't remember what else she needed. She began to look for other harmless plants, too, just in case they might help. Birch bark. Bundles of sumac berries, which stained her hands red. Buds and leaves of red clover. Fuzzy mullein.

She wandered toward the creek until something stopped her. It was a feeling more than anything else. Each tree was familiar, and she realized she was back in the birch grove, though she'd reached it from a different direction than usual. The grove where she met Tom. In just a few days, the leaves had thickened and changed.

Mara sat on a log, suddenly dizzy, and swatted mosquitos from her face.

All the mornings she'd come here, slipped away. The anticipation she felt each time. And there was something else she'd liked about the meetings, something hard to put a finger on—not the secrecy, exactly, but the control. The sense of being unowned. Not by Lenny, whose rules she only needed when they suited her. And not by Tom, either. He may have helped her, but she was the one who made that happen, wasn't she? She made him want to help her. Eating the protein bars felt less like he was feeding her and more like she had found a way to feed herself.

She had respected Tom. She would not have spoken twice to him anywhere else, and she thought him incompetent with women, but she regarded his incompetence as she might the efforts of a slow but diligent child. So what if he never dated again? Everyone had their faults. He was judgmental, but he had never hurt her, and he paid her in food for her attention. If it was true that he risked his job to do so, then he was brave. There was a way, in fact, that she thought Tom really did care about her. It made his disappearance all the more confusing, more so than the rest of the crew's.

In the urgency with Kyle, Mara had little time to wonder why the crew had disappeared. She focused only on the fact that they were gone. She had not liked them before, and she liked them even less now. Maybe they would come back; she hoped so, for Kyle's sake, although she was in no position to count on it. But Tom alone had helped her, and for that reason he was the one she let herself hate. He had been a waste of her respect. And now here she was, alone. Gathering random plants just for something to do.

She sat and looked at the birch. The trees grew up, not out, and so the grove towered, a cathedral of white trunks and a high ceiling of leaves. There were ferns, something like ivy carpeting the earth. The yellow dandelions had long since gone to puff.

A strange feeling came over Mara, a sense of almost-understanding, and she froze to hold her mind in place, trying to follow the thought. What did it mean, if Tom cared about her? Or if he cared about being the kind of person who might. The kind of person who wouldn't just abandon a girl.

Her eyes swept the grove. It looked normal. She tried to remember what they had talked about, meeting here, but even at the time she had not really paid attention. Then her eye lit on the mushroom tree, the cluster of conks that rose like steps up the trunk, and she felt herself stand and walk toward them.

Each mushroom was the size of half a plate, with a brown top and a tan belly. One of them had fallen from the tree and lay at its base.

No, it hadn't fallen. Conks didn't fall.

She turned it over. It was hard but springy, like old wood. The words scratched in the belly were scraggly but clear:

JUST IN CASE

And beneath them, an arrow. When she put the conk back where it had been, she saw that it pointed at the fallen log.

Mara went to the log and looked around it. It seemed normal enough, but now she saw a line of smooth dirt at the base, dirt that should be covered with grass and leaves.

Weeks ago she could have picked up the log by one end, simply lifted and moved it, but not anymore. She kicked it hard and hurt her foot. When she pushed against it, her sandals slid and she fell to the ground on her knees. Finally she found a strong fallen branch and, with leverage, was able to budge the trunk. Beetles and centipedes scurried off to better homes.

There it was, shiny, right underneath where she'd been sitting. Tom's gun. She opened the chamber and found it loaded.

When Mara got back to camp, Bullfrog eyed up the gun.

"Where'd you get that?"

"Crew camp," she said. "Under one of the cots. We must have missed it."

Bullfrog looked at her for a while. "Well," he said finally. "Glad you found it."

Mara put the gun on the shelf, beside the knife. Then she unloaded her plants. Fir and yarrow, clover, sumac berries, plantain, mullein—they looked less like medicine and more like ingredients in a child's potion. She took each plant and massaged it, breaking the needles and bending leaves until they bruised and the surfaces grew moist, and then put them all in the pot to boil.

She let them boil a long time. The water turned an almost incandescent red-brown and thickened like gravy. Mara scooped some into a cup and gave it to Kyle.

"Drink this," she said.

It tasted sour. She had tried it. Maybe it was the yarrow or the mullein. The taste was familiar and pinched her tongue. The texture gritty, like dissolved clay.

But Kyle didn't wince. He brought the cup to his mouth and drank it down like water. Then he held out the cup for more. Twice more she refilled it, and twice more he drank, until there was nothing left in the pot but a mound of soggy leaves.

Kyle didn't ask if the drink would help, and Mara was glad, because then she would have had to answer. It would help as much as anything, or as much as nothing. She felt angry again, too angry to speak, and she left the shelter so that Kyle wouldn't think her anger was aimed at him. Ashley was already in the lake, so Mara couldn't go there. Instead she hauled branches to the signal fires, and felt great satisfaction in raising the flames.

22

C ome out here!" called Bullfrog, in the morning. "Look at this!"

There was wonder in his voice and it gave Mara hope. She dropped the wood she was carrying and jogged into the woods, arriving at Bullfrog's side at the same time as Ashley. Everything seemed normal, quiet branches, quiet trees, and Mara felt disappointed until she looked down.

The fawn was almost perfectly camouflaged against the twigs and the dirt. It was no bigger than a cat. Curled in the dappled sunlight, long legs tucked beneath it, with a perfect curve of white specks on silky red-brown fur. Thin fluff at its neck, huge ears, eyelashes like feathers. Its white chin tucked to its chest. Like something from another world. Clean. Nothing like the world here.

Maybe nature knows when you're hungry, Mara thought, and knows when you have fish. Now that they had food, they could see the fawn. They were not a threat anymore, so they had earned the right. Or maybe the animals were coming back now that the crew was gone.

Now that the crew was gone. The ease of the words, the normalcy, brought a tangible flutter to her chest. But here was the fawn, perfect, before them. Here was a real and living thing.

"Is it orphaned?" said Ashley. She wasn't wearing her microphone anymore. Kyle was the only one who still did.

"No," said Bullfrog. "Its mother left it here. She'll come get it."

"Why did she leave it?"

"She thought it would be safe."

Ashley reached out her fingers and touched the fawn's back, tracing the fur from neck to tail. "When will she be back?"

"Dusk, probably. I don't know. Or when she's done eating."

"Can I pick it up?"

"I think that's fine."

Ashley wrapped her hands around the fawn's ribs and lifted it gently into her arms. The fawn relaxed against her. It placed its white chin on her shoulder and closed its eyes.

"It's trusting," said Mara.

"Never had a reason to be afraid," said Bullfrog. "Doesn't have the sense to be."

Mara wanted to hold the fawn herself. She imagined the feeling of cool fur on her own cheek. But she didn't want to pet the fawn while Ashley held it, and she didn't want to ask. She waited for Ashley to put the fawn down, to give the rest of them a turn, but Ashley started swaying, humming, and only held the fawn closer.

"I want to show Kyle," Ashley said finally.

Bullfrog had become the fawn's authority. As a hunter, he knew deer. "Let's mark the spot," he said. "So you can put it back right here. Where Mom can find it."

He placed a white stone where the fawn had lain, and arranged two sticks in an X beside it. It would be easy to come back and find the same place.

Of course Kyle knew facts about fawns. He propped himself up on his hands.

"It's a girl," he said. "Probably five or six days old. You see the spots? Most predators can't see color, so the spots help her blend into the forest floor." He gave the fawn his finger, and she began to suck. Then she let go, disappointed. She was anxious in the shelter, near the fire, with the smell of smoke. She kicked her legs, but Ashley held her tight.

"It's okay," said Ashley, petting her. Mara wondered if the fawn was as soft as she looked.

"It's time to bring her back," said Mara.

"Not yet," said Ashley. She went outside and sat on the grass, away from Bullfrog's vomit, which had dried into a crust. She put the fawn down, and it curled into a ball beside her. "See? She likes me."

The signal fires were smoldering. Mara went to the lake and lay down and closed her eyes. She imagined petting the fawn. She had seen fawns, of course, but never this young, never this close. She wondered if the deer she had seen long ago was the fawn's mother, and decided that it was. Maybe the doe had left her baby close to their camp on purpose, because she knew that other animals, predators, would stay away. Mara decided she was going to go pet the fawn, to feel for herself how soft it was. She went back to the clearing and crouched near it and touched the fawn's back.

It felt like satin, like water. The spots were even more perfect up close.

When Mara touched the fawn, Ashley looked up, and their eyes met. Mara's lungs grew tight. But then Ashley looked away, without any recognition in her eyes, and she pulled the fawn back into her lap and wrapped her arms around it even tighter.

Stupid, thought Mara. Stupid. She was nothing to Ashley. Just a prop for her story. She shouldn't have come over. As if she really needed to be reminded.

She tried to keep her voice steady. "It's time to bring the fawn back."

Bullfrog had come over, and Ashley turned to him. "Not yet. Please."

"We probably should," he said. "I wouldn't be surprised if Mom is watching us right now."

Mara looked out at the woods. When she looked back, Ashley had buried her face in the fawn's belly. The fawn blinked its long lashes.

"It's time," said Bullfrog gently.

no

Mara thought she had imagined the word. Bullfrog reached out to take the fawn from Ashley, but the moment his hand touched her, she bristled like she'd been shocked.

"No," Ashley said again.

"Well, soon," said Bullfrog.

"No." Her voice was more confident now. "I'm going to keep her. I'll take care of her."

"She's not an orphan."

"She's *not* an orphan. She's mine."

Mara felt dizzy again and sat down.

"She needs milk," said Bullfrog. "You got deer milk?"

"It's okay," said Ashley. "I'll figure it out. She already likes me."

She carried the fawn into the shelter, where Mara heard Kyle's voice, and then there was silence. When Mara came back later, she found Ashley feeding the fawn a mash of water and jam, scooping up fingerfuls for her to suck. By afternoon, the fawn toddled after Ashley wherever she went.

"YOU EVER THINK ABOUT DYATLOV?" SAID BULLFROG. IT WAS EVENING, IN THE shelter. Just past dark. The firelight flickered on the walls.

"Is that supposed to mean something to us?" said Mara.

"In Russia," said Bullfrog. "In the fifties, I guess. These climbers went up a mountain and disappeared. Real experienced mountaineers. When the search party found their tent, it was sliced open from the inside. They'd all run in different directions, wearing underwear, one boot. Barefoot. Their bodies were messed up. Cracked skulls, missing tongues. No survivors. They never figured out what did it."

Ashley petted her fawn.

"What's your point?" said Mara. "People do irrational things when they panic. Something flips in their brains." She'd heard of folks who got lost in the wilderness and crossed highways without realizing it. Or burned their own clothes for warmth. Or were found starved to death a mile from town.

"Sure," said Bullfrog. "But I'm not talking about mistakes. I'm talking about actual weird shit in the woods. You think about that?"

"Weird shit happens everywhere," said Mara. "You been to a city?"

"It was an avalanche," said Kyle softly. "At Dyatlov Pass." Mara startled at his voice. She didn't know he was awake.

"Sure," said Bullfrog. "*That* explains it."

"I'm just saying," said Kyle. "There aren't any avalanches here."

23

Kyle's foot turned grayish, and his face grew damp with sweat. The skin around his wound crackled like plastic, and the air above it felt warm. Sometimes he moaned, but mostly he lay back and took shallow breaths. He did not look down when Mara changed the bandage, though she was sure he could smell it. She breathed through her mouth in the shelter. No matter how many maggots she picked off, within hours there were always more.

"Fuck it," said Bullfrog. "I'm finding a way out." He was gone much of the time, venturing farther and farther in his scouting missions. But even when he came back, he kept his distance from the shelter. Mara was afraid to hope for what he'd find. She couldn't decide if she envied or resented him. Looking for help seemed far easier than staying with Kyle and Ashley, and when Bullfrog was scouting, she couldn't do the same.

Ashley sat in the meadow and petted her fawn in a beam

of golden light. Like a woman in a picture book, a princess or a witch.

"You have to cut it off," Kyle told Mara.

It had been six days since his fall.

"Don't be absurd," she said. "Someone could show up any second now. They're probably loading the helicopter. I'm not going to make things worse."

She gave him tea, and he drank it, but he didn't stop.

"Look at it," he said.

She didn't want to look at it.

"Look at it," he said.

Mara unwrapped the bandage, which draped only loosely now over the wound. She had covered the raw flesh with a mullein leaf, and Kyle winced when she tugged to peel it off.

The wound had grown. It was deeper now, as if it were a living thing, eating itself, and she thought she saw a tendon in the depths of it. There were more maggots, though she had cleaned them out recently, and she plucked them off with tweezers and dropped them in the fire. The wound was so thick with yellow pus that it was hard to tell where the maggots ended and the pus began.

"Maybe more vodka," she said.

"No," he said. "You have to cut off the infection. It's the only way to keep it from spreading. But the vodka will come in handy."

"You're not making sense."

"Dib dib dib," said Kyle.

"See?"

"It's from Scouts," he said. "It means do your best."

Mara was doing her best, and she could not do any more.

"Just listen," he said. "Hear me out, okay?"

She didn't want to listen, but she did.

"I think I should get very drunk on vodka," he said, "and Bullfrog and Ashley should pin me down. You should be the one to do it."

"Why not Bullfrog?"

"He wouldn't," said Kyle, and Mara knew he was right. "You have to let them handle the top half and you can handle my leg. I'll probably try to fight them, but I'm pretty sure they can hold me down."

"Please stop telling me this."

"I'm not telling you for fun. I'm telling you because it's important." Kyle was trembling, but his voice was steady. "My foot," he continued. "I know you're pretending it's okay, but it's bad. You know how infections work. I don't have long before it hits my blood. If it hasn't yet. So you'll need to make a very tight tourniquet around my calf. Then find where the swelling is and cut beyond that. Make sure you're past any redness, and if you're not sure, cut higher. Sanitize the knife, and cover your mouth so you're not breathing on me while you do it. Try to cut through the muscle quickly, so I don't have much time to fight you. You're going to have to saw through my tibia and fibula. Otherwise you could try to break them off, but I think sawing is better. If you heat the knife in the fire, you might be able to cauterize blood vessels as you go."

"Even if this was a reasonable idea," Mara said, "and not a terrible one, you'd still end up with a whole new wound to get infected. A much worse one. And you'd have no fucking leg."

"It might buy me a few days," he said.

"Do you hear yourself?"

"I feel it, Mara."

"I think you have blood poisoning already and it's gone to your head."

"Maybe."

Mara felt suddenly very angry that Bullfrog and Ashley had left her to deal with this.

"So tell me," she said, "Mr. Expert, how many field amputations have you performed?"

"Eight," he said. "Maybe nine."

"Did they go as well as your deadfall traps?"

"You're joking, but I'm serious."

"You joked first."

"I'm allowed to. It's my foot."

"Well, I wish you wouldn't."

"Mara," he said.

"What now?"

His hand found hers, and he was shaking harder. She squeezed his hand back.

"I'm scared," he said.

That was what chilled her most. Not the conversation but those two words, the tremor that reached his voice at last.

"I know," she said. "But you shouldn't be. You're gonna be okay."

For some reason she imagined her father there, in the shelter beside them, and the words in her mouth were his. "It's a game, remember?" said her father. "This is all a game. We're just playing, to see what happens. If it gets too real then the game is off. That's the rules."

"You think they're really watching? They're coming?"

Neither of them believed it.

"Yes," Mara said. "I don't just think it. I know that it's true. If the game's going on, that means they know we're safe.

There's probably a doctor watching us on a live screen right now, gauging when to step in." She waved at the air. "Hey, Doctor! Thanks for looking out for us. Shit's scary, but we're trusting your judgment on this."

"I'm tired," said Kyle.

"I know," said Mara. "You should probably rest."

It had been half an hour since Kyle's last nap. He spent more time now sleeping than awake.

"I have to pee," she said. "I'll be outside."

Outside it was bright and warm. Jays swooped through the clearing, and she heard the rat-tat of a woodpecker in the trees. She started to walk.

Her dad was gone now. A trick of a mind at the end of its rope. She wondered why he'd come. She had thought she was angry at Bullfrog and Ashley, but actually she was angry at him, or maybe just angry, anger that settled wherever she turned her gaze. Angry at herself, and at the trees. Angry at the sky that brought them there and the lake that caught them. Angry that she had ever left Salem and moved to the country, a move that started the chain of events that led to this moment. Anger that somehow her parents wanted a life like this and made it true.

That wasn't fair. Was it?

She had been groomed for survival her whole life, and still she was failing. I give up, she thought. Take everything. Take my knife. Take my car. Take my money. Take me anywhere but here.

Take me to the suburbs.

Take me to school.

Take me wherever it is that normal people go. Teach me however it is that they live. Because they did, didn't they?

They just lived. They went to grocery stores and to the doctor. They went to movies and the gym. They went to work in the morning and home at night. They had pets, normal pets, and they sat on the couch and watched television and judged the people on-screen. Probably that was fun. She should try it. She should sit on a couch and eat popcorn and make pronouncements about people she didn't know, as if she had the right, as if her opinion on them mattered. There was a reason that most people lived like that, and she should join them.

It all seemed very obvious and she was stupid to have missed it for so long. There was no reason to make life harder. There was no reason to make life hard at all. It was impossible enough already.

She had walked a long way and circled back, and come to the creek, and walked out on the peninsula of stones, kicking them as she walked. Sending each one skittering as far as she could.

That was when she smelled it. Strong, indistinguishable. Like fish and blood.

Like fish and blood. How strange. She remembered the smell, but not where it came from. It came from within her, she thought. And then she heard the voice, and she thought it was in her mind. Coming to her like music through water, garbled and distant. Her name in Ashley's mouth. "Mara. Don't move."

Everyone was talking to her. Everyone she loved.

But it wasn't Ashley. It was Bullfrog.

"Don't move."

It was a hiss, but it came like a punch. Brought Mara back to the world.

She saw him at the edge of the water, eight or ten yards

downstream. Staring at her. He raised a finger and pointed. And when she turned her head, she knew what she would see.

The bear was bigger now. Fatter, glossy, thick fur catching the light. Big head held low. She pushed air through her mouth so her lips fluttered. The bear looked past Mara intently, and Mara turned to follow her gaze.

She knew what she would see there, too.

The cub sat behind her, on the end of the gravel spit. His face was twitching. Ears flicking, nose to the wind. Alert.

All Mara had learned about mother bears was to stay away. Not to get near their cubs, and to never come between them. To avoid the situation at any cost. She had never learned what to do if it had already happened.

Should she raise her arms, look big?

No, that would be worse. That would make her seem a threat.

Maybe she could get to the cub somehow. Pass it. Get it to pass her. But that would mean stepping toward it, which would also make her a threat.

Mara shifted her weight slightly. Testing the movement.

The bear rose to her back feet, as easily as a bird taking flight. She let out a bark, deep and rumbling, and every hair on Mara's body rose at once.

She should jump in the water.

It was the only way. The only solution. If Mara could get to the edge of the spit without triggering the bear. If she could somehow make clear that she was only getting away. That she would not come back. That she would never come back again.

Mara moved her foot. Just her toes, an inch toward the water. The bear barked again, and this time it was louder. This time it ate the world.

Mara made herself small, shrunken. Crouched. Pulled in against her very bones. Her eyes down, her empty palms up, although she knew that was a human gesture, a gesture that meant nothing, a gesture her body found when it had nothing else to say. She had never felt so human.

And then Mara's anger came back again, hitting her like a wall. Now she was angry at the bear. Angry at the bear for her violent irrational drive to protect her child, angry that Mara was at risk when she had done nothing wrong, when she had not meant to hurt her, she had not meant to hurt anyone ever, she had only meant to walk to the creek, she had only meant to walk away.

Well, thought Mara. This will go one way or another.

She stood up and closed her eyes.

A sound rose, a sound that may or may not have come from her own head. A rush that turned into a scream, a bang, an explosion. And as quickly as it had come, the sound ended. Mara opened her eyes.

Blood spurted from the mama bear's neck. She shook and it flew from her, a red sprinkler, and she turned in lumbering, frantic circles, looking for the source of the pain. For the third time, Mara knew what she would see before she saw it.

Downstream, Bullfrog lowered the gun.

24

Bullfrog and Mara butchered the bear while her cub watched. Her guts sloshed from her belly, steaming, and stained the river stones. She seemed smaller now. Maybe three hundred pounds. Two-fifty gutted. The size of a large man, nothing more; the size of the man in front of you in line at the bank. Her black hair coarse and thick, as long as Mara's fingers, and the skin beneath it almost translucent. She had dandruff.

The cub watched. He was not so young. A yearling. Maybe he would live.

The bear's heart was still beating. Not in her chest, but in Bullfrog's hand. The chambers twitching on their own, still struggling to push blood. Bullfrog put the heart aside.

They cut from her flank and her thigh, long thin strips to dry and smoke, and they didn't worry about the smell, because what bear would they draw with the scent of meat, who would come? Nobody was coming. Nobody was coming, and so they would eat.

"Will he live?" Mara asked Bullfrog, of the cub. For all she'd done in the woods, she had never been a hunter. She didn't know these things.

"I think he will," said Bullfrog. "If he can find enough food by fall."

Now they had enough food. Mara didn't ask Bullfrog where he'd gone or what he found. The answer was obvious: wherever he'd gone, however far he had walked, he had found nothing. It was better not to make him say it aloud.

They cooked tenderloins on the pot lid, and the meat was good. Thick and dark, if a little stringy. Mara sliced the edges from a pheasants' back mushroom and seared them in the leftover juice, a rubbery approximation of fries. They mixed scoops of jam in cups of hot water to make a thin, sweet drink for dessert. They sat by the fire, the four of them, and passed a packet of ramen seasoning for flavor, tapping sprinkles of orange powder onto the vegetables and the meat.

After dinner they played cards. Go Fish. Kyle got ahead with fours and sevens and he held the lead. The game was good because it was simple, and none of them were feeling smart. When it wasn't Kyle's turn, he closed his eyes. Ashley petted her fawn with one hand and held her cards with the other. Her fawn had grown bony, and its ears curled back.

Between games, Mara shuffled. She had heard once that most arrangements in a deck of cards had never been made before and would never be made again. She didn't believe it then, but now she did.

Kyle didn't mention amputation again.

In the morning, Bullfrog built a smoker, and the air filled with the smell of smoked bear. Rich and persistent, a scent that stuck to your skin. Mara went back to the carcass, where the flies were so lethargic that she could pick them off with her fingers, and cut a thick sheet of fat from under the fur. She rendered it on the outdoor fire into oil, and they rubbed the oil into their dry and flaking skin. Mara massaged it into Kyle's arms, his good leg. They all reeked with the smell of it. They got the cards and played another hand. The cards were greasy, too.

"Do you have any threes?" Mara asked Bullfrog. Then, in the same thought, "Why did you come here?"

At one time it would have felt rude to ask. Now it felt like nothing. His was the only story she didn't know.

"I thought my daughter might see the show," Bullfrog said. "And then maybe she would talk to me again."

But he didn't have any threes.

THEY TOOK TURNS WATCHING KYLE. IT WAS HARD TO DO FOR LONG ALONE. WATCH-ing him suffer. Sometimes he sank into delirium, mumbling and once screaming, and sometimes he'd be clear for minutes or even hours. Streaks of red traced up his leg and past his thigh. "If it gets worse, kill me," he told Mara, and made her promise that if he died, they would leave and find safety. Two hours later, he gripped her wrist with both hands and made her promise to keep him alive.

Mara came back after Bullfrog's turn and found Kyle alone, asleep, with the gun resting beside him. There was no way he could have reached it himself from the shelf. Bullfrog must have left it there.

She caught Bullfrog by the lake. She was livid. People knew where they were. People were coming. People didn't abandon people to die in the woods.

It was the first time she saw Bullfrog angry. "I didn't leave the gun there so he would kill himself," he said. "Jesus, Mara. I left it there so he could make his own damn decision to live."

"You gave him a gun so he *wouldn't* shoot himself?"

"Yes," said Bullfrog. "So he could choose not to."

"That's not a thing."

"Imagine being him," said Bullfrog. "If that was you, you'd want the same choice. Give the man power over one damn thing in his life right now."

As much as Mara hated to admit it, Bullfrog was right. She would want the same. From then on, when they left the shelter, they left the gun at Kyle's side.

AT NIGHT, WHEN THEY WERE TOO TIRED TO DO ANYTHING ELSE, WHEN THEY WERE too tired to deny the obvious, they talked again and again through what might have happened to the crew. Every scenario they could imagine. Sometimes they guessed big: nuclear war, apocalypse. Something that wiped out everyone in the world but them. It was comforting to imagine the outrageous; it made things less real. But mostly they went small. A plane crash, Bullfrog insisted. It had to be. It was simple. Float plane down, everyone dies.

"There'd be search parties," said Ashley.

"Somebody'd really be looking for you right now?" He shook his head. "Bet you told your folks you'd be gone for months. I don't know about you, but I don't have anyone counting the days."

They looked at Kyle. He was shivering.

"He does," said Mara. "He has family."

"And you?" said Bullfrog.

Ashley tossed a stick into the fire. "Yes. And the crew has family, too."

"You think those camera guys are calling home?" said Bullfrog. "They said, 'Hey, Mom, don't worry about me for a while, I'm going off grid.'"

"What about the pilot?" said Ashley.

"He's a hermit. Flies his own plane. Has a tomcat who's been waiting years for the chance to eat him. Cat's probably starved to death now."

"Bullfrog," said Mara.

"I'm just saying, it's not impossible."

"Okay," said Ashley, in a tight, small voice. "A plane crash."

Her arms formed a perfect ring around the fawn. It was crumpled and skeletal, and one ear drooped over Ashley's wrist. Mara didn't feel anything when she saw it, except sadness that Kyle had to see it, too. But at least he was asleep.

Mara looked at the gun. She didn't want to talk. It was best to let the story lie. But her mouth moved anyway.

"It wasn't a plane crash," she said. "Tom left me the gun. He knew he'd be gone."

She watched from the corner of her eye, but Ashley didn't look up.

"He say anything else?" said Bullfrog.

"A note. 'Just in case.'"

Bullfrog stared into the fire. "Maybe he quit the job. Maybe Lenny caught him sneaking and fired him, eh? And he wanted to help you before he left. Still doesn't mean there wasn't a plane crash. Maybe he tried to help you out, and then he died."

"I don't want to think about this," said Ashley.

"Okay," said Bullfrog. "We'll take a break."

He was quiet for a while. Mara closed her eyes.

"Hear me out," Bullfrog whispered to the darkness. "Aliens." But no one answered.

In her half dreams, it was the last word Mara heard before Ashley's scream woke her. She reached past the fire and felt the fawn's body, hard and cold to the touch.

Ashley seemed less sad than disgusted. She shoved the fawn from her and ran out of the shelter to retch. Nobody followed. She slumped in the doorway, her figure a blacker black than the night itself.

The fawn seemed peaceful now. Bullfrog gutted it, and in the morning butchered what was left. There wasn't much, but there was skin Mara could dry or tan, which would at least give her something to do. She had not tanned the bear hide. It was too much. But the fawn she could handle, and if Kyle woke up he could criticize her tanning technique, which would both please him and pass the time. *Every animal*, she imagined him saying, *has a brain big enough to tan its own hide.*

Bullfrog made an organ stew from the heart and tongue and the tiny liver, chopped into small bits. He had carved each of the survivors a bowl and a spoon to go with the cups. When they ate the fawn, Ashley ate it, too.

Mara waited for Ashley to cry or gag, but she didn't. She took a spoonful of stew and chewed. Then she swallowed. Then she took another spoonful and chewed too many times before swallowing. Like an actor chewing. Like she was chewing gum. She swallowed, and Mara watched the bulge as the food slid down her throat. Without expression, Ashley reached for a third bite.

They finished the pot in one meal. The fawn had been young and starving. It wasn't much to eat.

Kyle didn't wake up. The air around his body was hot, and in sleep he whimpered and moaned. He had soiled himself. They cleaned and cushioned him with grass and leaves.

25

After the fawn died, something changed. Mara tried to hide it. But each time she came into the shelter, she stopped hoping Kyle would be better. She started hoping that he would be dead.

Then one horror, at least, would be over.

She hated herself for the thought, and did her best to ignore it. She tried to scrape the fawn's hide, but it was delicate and tore easily, and when she had made a handful of coin-sized tears in the tissue-thin leather she gave up and threw it in the lake. When she wasn't checking on Kyle, she walked, though she didn't let herself go far, always circling within hearing distance of camp. She found a waterfall over mossy stones that once would have struck her as beautiful. The mist cast rainbows. But beauty didn't strike her anymore.

When Mara got back, Kyle lay and sweat and shook. He was alone. He was mumbling. Mara felt faint, like her lungs had shrunk to half their size, and even so she couldn't fill them. She found Ashley outside, sitting by the signal fires, though the flames had burned low.

"He's bad," said Mara. It was hard to breathe.

Ashley closed her eyes.

"I know you're going through something," said Mara. "I do. And you lost your—your pet, right? I know that's sad." It was hard to say the words, but she managed them.

"I killed my pet," said Ashley.

"It was an accident."

"No," said Ashley. "Don't do that. I knew."

"I don't know what you want me to say," said Mara. "Kyle's alone. Can you sit with him?"

"I needed something nice," said Ashley. "Just for a minute."

"I can't do it," said Mara.

Ashley opened her eyes.

"He needs someone and I can't do it," said Mara. "Okay? I can't sit in the shelter and give Kyle what he needs and I don't know where Bullfrog is and I can't just . . ." She stopped, tried to breathe, but the air caught in her throat. "I can't leave him like that."

"He goes looking for help," said Ashley. "Bullfrog."

"Yes," said Mara. "I would also love to be looking for help. How convenient. Anywhere but here."

"He can't stand it," said Ashley.

"None of us can stand it," said Mara.

Ashley nodded.

"Kyle needs you," said Mara. "Please."

"He needs something nice," said Ashley. She stood up; she shivered, and it seemed to shake something free. Her voice was not hers, exactly, but it was steady. "Somebody has to do it."

Like a ghost, like something superhuman, she went through the shelter door.

Mara sat in the yellow glow of the sun and listened, as if to a radio program, while Ashley talked to Kyle. Flies crawled over her mouth, and she didn't bother to brush them away. There would just be more. She felt like her skin was humming. Like her chest was full of smoke.

Ashley's voice cracked at first, trailed off on certain words, but somehow it always started again. She told Kyle about himself, about his life and family, about the future he wanted and planned to have. Mara didn't know when Ashley had learned those things. But then she remembered that they used to talk, Ashley and Kyle, that they were the social ones, the ones whose tasks kept them close to camp. Her with the water and him with the traps. Maybe they were even friends.

"You have three siblings," Ashley told Kyle. "And you're the oldest. You earned your Eagle Scout rank by building a bridge in the woods. It was two miles from the nearest road, and you hauled the wood there yourself. You used to work at a pizza restaurant. You were good at throwing dough.

"You have a plan when you leave here. You promised your little sister that wherever the show brought you, you'd bring her back someday. You'd show her how you lived and how to catch food and stuff. She's already making her outfit for the premiere. She's embroidering it with flowers and leaves. She showed you her sketches the day you left. She's going to wear it to the airport when you come home.

"You want to be a pilot. You're going to use the prize money for flying school. A commercial pilot, like your grandpa. You'd like to see the world from above . . ."

Ashley kept going.

The buzzing in Mara's skin had started to fade. She didn't want to listen anymore. She walked.

It was the end of June. She knew it was the end of June because she had taken over Kyle's calendar, scratching a mark on the eave each night, and now there were forty-two marks. Six weeks.

The day they should have left.

It was dangerous to think about. Six weeks here—it felt more like a decade. She let herself imagine what would have happened if nothing had happened. If the game had stayed a game, and the show a show.

Where they could have been. Should have been.

There'd be some dramatic departure, of course. Lenny wouldn't be able to resist. Have them climb a mountain again, boosting each other over boulders, or maybe they'd do a reverse of the first day, swim out into the lake and climb a knotted rope into helicopters above.

There'd be final interviews. They'd wear their ragged clothing, looking weary but triumphant. The cameras would coax out the soundbites. Full sentences. Present tense. Until *Civilization*, we never knew what we were capable of. Now we've tackled our demons. Tackled nature and won. We've learned the importance of other people. We'll never take anything for granted ever again.

There'd be footage of family members waiting. Not Mara's probably, or Bullfrog's, but Ashley's mom and sister and all of Kyle's siblings, cheering for the reunion in the lobby of some posh lodge. Waitresses in button-down shirts and a moose mount above the stone fireplace, with a Stetson hanging off one antler. They would get to bathe, scrub off the dirt until they were clean, brush their hair, put on their old or their fancy clothes. Kyle in chinos. Ashley in an eyelet dress. "You're too thin," her family would exclaim, but of course that was part of the triumph: the discipline, the fortitude and the restraint.

There'd be food, certainly. Lenny had mentioned that once: that on the day they got out, they could request any meal that they wanted. Early on, Bullfrog said his would be fish fry, but Mara wondered if he would change his tune now that they ate fish every day. She'd ask for lasagna, the dripping sauce and thick, chewy noodles, that rich and crumbling ricotta. And Kyle—

It was best not to dream.

How worthless they must have seemed to Lenny. Symbols to be plied with money and cheese.

Maybe it was the fact that Mara was avoiding the shelter. How much calmer she felt, away from it. Or maybe it was the thought of food, of safety. The thought that it should have been today. Even in a sick world where this was still a murderous show, it should and would have been today. But Mara moved with a purpose that she hadn't felt in some time. To the crew camp, the supply tent, where she gathered more flares. She tucked them into the back of her bra and made her way to the big maple.

There had to be a way out. Maybe it was up.

Up close, the tree seemed a harder climb than it had from even a short distance. Countless boughs, but scale had dwarfed the space between them. Even the closest were four feet apart, and on opposite sides of the thick trunk. Kyle was a stronger climber than Mara realized. He had made it look easy. Or not easy, but doable.

If it was doable, she could do it, too. One limb at a time.

The first was at Mara's chest level. With a running start,

she heaved her upper body across it, landing hard on her gut. Caught her breath and pulled her legs up, scraping against the bark. The limb was wide, and she could stand on it comfortably, holding the trunk, though already she felt too high off the ground. She decided that height was just an illusion. Wherever she stood was the new ground. The ground would rise up the tree beneath her, ready to catch her if she fell.

The next limbs were closer together, with smaller branches for handholds and steps along the way. Almost like climbing a ladder, though Mara heard and felt cracks as she moved. She climbed quickly, without hesitating to think, until she reached another wide bough, and there she leaned against the trunk to give her heart rate a chance to slow. Her hands were shaking, and she felt the trunk itself swaying in the breeze. She hadn't noticed a breeze from the ground.

No, she told herself. The ground was right beneath her feet. She needed to believe it rose with her, that if she fell she would not fall, that there was nothing to worry about, no reason to panic and freeze. She felt for the flares, and they were still tucked against her skin. She kept climbing.

When she was halfway up the tree, a stick broke off in her hand, and though she grabbed the trunk in time to catch herself, she heard the stick crash down, bouncing off limbs for a long time. The sound shrank as it fell away.

Mara climbed. She reached the point where Kyle had struggled, a huge gap of space, and as she let her body swing across it, her mind switched off completely. There were no thoughts or feelings, no hope that she would catch herself or fear that she might not; she swung across the space and caught herself, and her body rose higher, and she no longer cared about anything at all. She would have climbed forever to stay in that relief. Until she reached the top fork of the trunk, and straddled it, and then she looked down.

She was so far from the ground.

Their world in miniature. Trees covering the earth like moss, and the lake self-contained, blue as the summer sky. The creek wound out of sight, leisurely, lingering in oxbows and pools. No rush to the inevitable. The bear's carcass on the gravel bar just a black mark covered in crows. Every now and then they stretched their tiny wings.

The tree swayed, sweeping from side to side with the wind, but it felt like she was the only thing still, and the earth swayed beneath her like waves at sea. The clearing, the shelter, the coals from the signal fires, seemed more like a diorama than the real thing. A museum exhibit made of twigs. How quaint that they lived their lives like that and thought that they mattered. In the distance, shimmering, she saw the lake by crew camp, which also didn't matter, which was just as small and lost as they all were. She wanted out.

She pulled the first flare from her bra. It was an orange plastic tube about the size of a pen, but thicker, and she peeled off the paper wrapping. She had never fired a flare before, but it seemed simple enough. When she unscrewed the container, a little chain dropped out the bottom, and she understood that she was to point and pull it hard.

A boom like a gunshot. A blinding flash. Smoke pouring from her hands. The light rose high for a long time, red and weightless, shrinking into the pale sky.

The first shot was for Kyle. Come find him. Before we are all like him. Save him. Please somebody come to us and help.

The second shot was for the fawn. The stupid innocent fawn.

The third shot was for the rest of them. It echoed.

Save Ashley, thought Mara, who I don't hate, who I never hated, who came here knowing what she had to do, who is broken and fucked up and ambitious and lets herself want in ways I have never wanted anything but her.

Save Bullfrog, who is doing all of this so that one person might look at him just once more.

Save me, because I came here to have choices for once, and now I deserve to make them. We all needed a way out. We all needed a way in.

"You motherfuckers!" she screamed. Louder than she ever had, until her voice cracked and her throat burned. "Come save us!"

But there was only silence. Just the swaying of the earth below, and the branches and leaves dancing around her, and the gradual awareness of her arms and legs scraped raw from the bark. Her wrists itched. Her left hip throbbed. Between gusts she could hear the creek.

She was too high up.

Mara climbed down slowly. Inch by inch, time stretching around her. Feeling with her toes for each solid branch, pressing twice to make sure it wouldn't break beneath her. Everything trembling, though she felt strong. She couldn't stop shaking. Halfway down she stopped to catch her breath, and when she had caught it enough she continued to descend.

At the base of the tree, she lay on her stomach and pressed her face into the ground. Ants and insects crawled in the grass, which had grown tall and thick. Her heartbeat pounded in her ears. She searched for the spent flares and gathered them and put them in her pocket and started toward camp. She didn't want to litter.

When Mara got to the shelter, Ashley stood before it with her arms at her side. Like she was screwing up the courage to go in. Then Mara came closer and saw the gun in her hand, the spray of blood across her face.

"He asked me to," Ashley said.

Mara ran to her as she collapsed.

26

Bullfrog came shortly. He must have heard the shot, the flares. He took in the two women, clinging together. Then he went into the shelter, and when he came out he caught Mara's eye and shook his head.

"You don't want to see that." The way he said it, he might have been talking to himself.

Mara didn't want to see it, but she had to. She went into the shelter and went out again.

Bullfrog was right. She wished she hadn't. She stared into the blue sky, trying to get the image from her head. She closed her eyes and saw it on her eyelids. Kyle's hand outstretched on the grass mat, palm down, layers of freckles and dirt. Dark curves under cracked nails.

They sat on the grass for a long time, and finally the silence came around to a place where they could talk. They had all become very calm.

Mara was thinking about Kyle, but she wasn't thinking

about Kyle. She couldn't think about him directly. She thought about his hero, Chris McCandless, instead.

"Isn't it weird," Mara said, "that McCandless used to be a person?"

"Like that he was alive?" said Ashley.

"No, not like that. But, like, that he was a person. He went to the bathroom and ate cereal and had thoughts, and probably most of them no one ever heard. And that's all gone now, but people act like they know him."

It seemed to her now that the more people acted like they knew you, the less you existed. They built you a shell and didn't care if it fit. People talked like they knew McCandless—hadn't she?—but the thing they talked about wasn't him. They all just pretended it was. And nobody stopped them, because who would?

When Mara was a kid, before she left the suburbs, her mom took her to a puppet show at a public library. The actors set up a whole stage in the children's room, and the kids sat cross-legged to watch. The puppets danced and talked, and behind them, making them move, were actors dressed in black. They weren't even hiding. They just stood there with their arms out, and when the puppets got animated they moved their arms faster. Mara knew that she was supposed to ignore them, to pretend the puppets were real and the people weren't. But she couldn't do it. She kept staring at the actors. There was a woman with long white hair who widened her eyes each time her puppet spoke, but her mouth didn't move at all. The whole thing struck Mara as horrible. She couldn't remember the storyline they were acting out. Even at the time it seemed beside the point.

Eventually she started crying, loud enough that others in

the audience turned to look. One of the puppets broke from script to say, "Little girl, what's wrong?" which only made Mara cry harder. Her mom rushed her out, apologizing, and they went for ice cream instead.

Mara hadn't thought of that show in years, maybe a decade, and she wasn't sure why the memory came to her then. She thought maybe it was how the cameras had made her feel. Like she was the puppet master, and Mara on-screen the puppet, rushing around for her little tasks, and everyone had agreed to pretend that that was the real story. Even if the audience could see the real Mara somehow—the woman who needed money, who was lost, who cheated on her boyfriend and couldn't even bring herself to care, because she cared so little for anything she'd left behind—they'd wish they hadn't. They'd pretend her away. Because they came for a performance, a story, with all the comfort a story entailed, the promise of beginning and middle and end. They came for entertainment. They came to watch her dance.

That was how Mara felt about McCandless, now that she thought about it. Except it seemed sadder, because he was dead. Everyone talked about the story, the performance, and not the man making the figure move. And that seemed like a second death somehow. Like every time they ignored the figure in black, he died a little more. And his creation, this dancing doll, this subject of campfire debate, this inspiration to Boy Scouts in Indiana, spun faster and faster.

She wondered if, like Kyle, McCandless had wanted to die. Or if, like Kyle, he had wanted to live.

There was some part of Kyle, Mara thought, that wanted to make a puppet desperately. That was why he came here, wasn't it? To make a performance of who he wanted to be, triumphant and fearless and wise. To come to agreement with the audience about who he really was, a character for them to root for and for him to become.

This camp was the stage Kyle had chosen, the set he'd built for himself. Maybe someday someone would come here to see the place where he'd spent his last days. A pilgrimage. This is where he ate, they might say. This is where he boiled water. This is where he set his traps. Do you see the lake? That's where he bathed. Do you see this tree? He climbed it.

"We should leave him here," said Mara. "I think that's what he'd want. He was proud of this camp and he was proud to be here."

"We could burn the shelter," said Ashley. "The whole thing."

That made sense, too. Flames for the closing curtain.

Mara had understood from the moment she saw the blood, they had all understood, that they were going to leave. It was the only option. It was nice that Kyle had once said so himself. It made Mara feel like they'd be honoring his wishes rather than abandoning him, and she wondered now if that was why he said it in the first place—not giving instructions, but permission. She had not previously ascribed much emotional insight to Kyle, but dying brought out the wisdom in everyone. Or maybe it just earned them the benefit of the doubt.

This camp had belonged to the four of them. Now they were three, and it wasn't theirs. It was time to go. If they found other people, they'd be saved. If they didn't, they'd be fucked. They might as well be fucked somewhere new.

They moved in silence, the three of them like arms and legs of the same creature, moving through dusk and into darkness. Gathering all the wood they had left, everything they had collected, and piling it around the outside of the shelter, the dry moss and the bark walls. Time had compacted the layers of the roof into one dense and brittle object. How dry the shelter was, after weeks of toasting from the fire within. How ready it was to burn.

Finally they had arranged the wood in a massive pyre. The shelter itself almost small in the center, like a child's toy. Lit gold in the setting sun.

Ashley walked to the doorway and slipped inside. She came out with an armload of belongings and dumped them on the grass, knife and pot and ramen and cards and flashlight and meat. Everything they owned together. Then she went back in.

She was gone for a long time. Mara thought she'd come back with a burning log, something to light the pyre from the outside in. But instead she came out with the bow drill. She gave it to Bullfrog, who crouched to rub the sticks. Just when he had built up a line of smoke, his hand shook. The bow flipped and clattered to the ground.

"He just had to pick a bow drill," said Mara. "He couldn't resist."

"It never runs out," said Bullfrog. "With a lighter, matches, when you use 'em up, you're screwed. Bow drill lasts forever."

Mara knelt beside him and took the other end of the bow. Together they pushed back and forth, back and forth. Finding a rhythm, rubbing the sticks together until smoke poured from their hands. She blew the coal into a flame.

They plied the flame with pine needles and birch bark and fatwood until it spread, until fire licked the panels of bark on either side of the shelter door. It took a long time for the shelter to catch. For minutes it only blackened. But once it did, the fire rose quickly. Soon the shelter was ablaze with flames six or seven feet high, casting a ring like daylight on the three survivors. Mara thought of Kyle inside it. She thought of his carved calendar burning to ashes beside him.

There was something familiar in the smoke, and it wasn't until Mara's mouth watered that she recognized the smell of grilled meat. She backed up until she couldn't smell it, noticed Bullfrog do the same. Ashley stared into the fire, her expression like the dead themselves. Mara touched her shoulder and pulled her back, and Ashley let herself be guided.

Bullfrog's lips were moving, and Mara realized he must be praying. The same words again and again. She sat down. She couldn't tell if she was crying. Her face was hot from the fire, too hot for tears, but she needed the warmth of it, couldn't bear to back farther away. Though the night air was warm, too. The fire hissed, cracked, sent up sprays of sparks to the waiting stars. Maybe this funeral wasn't for Kyle, she thought. Maybe it was for all of them. The only one they'd ever get.

Maybe Kyle, more than any of them, knew what he was getting into. Maybe he wanted it. Maybe that was a terrible thing to think of a child.

They didn't sleep all night, just sat and watched the flames. Watched them sink into glowing coals the size of boulders, then simmer in a dark mound. The morning came red like the fire itself.

"It seems to me the beautiful uncut hair of graves," said Mara.

"What's that mean?" asked Ashley.

"I'm not sure," Mara said. Though she had her ideas.

THEY TOOK STOCK OF THEIR BELONGINGS. A BUNDLE OF SMOKED BEAR MEAT AND some dried trout. Six bottles from crew camp, which they filled with water. The wind-up flashlight, which was a piece of crap. Knife, axe, lighter, bow drill just in case. They wrapped what they had in canvas bundles. They left the gun by the shelter, because it was heavy and out of bullets. They left the cameras in the trees.

Their first steps felt strange. Walking through a place they knew so well, knowing they would never see it again. What else was there to do?

They had to choose a direction. They walked along the lakeshore and found the creek that fed from the far side. After a while, another creek joined from the right, and now they walked beside a river. They would follow water; wherever it flowed, so would they. In this way, they hoped, they would not end up where they had started. Mara wondered if it was true that all rivers reach the sea. She wondered if this river had a name.

The river curled on itself, back and forth, and the banks were steep. The survivors scrambled, ducking through the trees, stumbling over roots, too tired to guard their faces from the branches that whipped back on them and stung.

They stopped often. Every few minutes, holding tree trunks, or crouching with their foreheads to their knees. Even with the ramen, the cookies, and the meat, they were weary. They were half people, worn thin. When Mara stood, her ears filled with the hum of a thousand bees. Her pulse pounded in her eyeballs, in every inch of her skin. They sat to sip from their bottles. They had walked an impossible distance, over an impossible period of time. It was probably less than two miles.

Bullfrog climbed down the bank and stepped into the river. Waves rose around his calves. To his right, the water darkened in a deeper channel. "It's better in the water. We can walk faster."

Mara slid down after him, waded into the shallow edge. The cold was a balm on her feet. The riverbed was rocky, cast with dancing light. She felt Ashley behind her.

But when Mara stepped forward, her foot slipped on a rock. For a split second she thought she'd fall. The river stones were slick as ice.

"I don't know about this," said Mara.

"It's fine," said Bullfrog.

Ashley waded past her. One careful step, then another.

"Wait," said Mara.

They both stopped.

"It just seems dangerous," said Mara. "Walking in the water. It would be easy to fall."

"Relax," said Bullfrog. "We'll be careful. Maybe we'll actually make some progress."

"Yeah, unless someone breaks their leg."

"It does seem faster," said Ashley.

Mara hesitated. The river was easy; there were no branches to push through, no logs to clamber over. Just a smooth and open path. But all they needed was one loose stone, one unexpected hole. One moment of lost balance. Even a shallow current could push them down. A sprained ankle, a broken foot, and—

Bullfrog took a swig from his bottle. "You coming?"

Just one more broken body. And then what? A fever. An infection. The sweating and waiting. The screaming. Who would be next? Bullfrog? Ashley? Mara herself?

"No," said Mara. "We'll walk on the bank. It's safer."

"It'll be fine," said Bullfrog.

"I'm not asking," said Mara.

Nobody moved. Ashley wasn't looking at either of them.

The water slid past, smooth, unhurried. Always flowing.

"Are you listening to me?" said Mara. She struggled to keep her voice calm, reasonable. "We can't get hurt out here. We can't afford to take chances."

"Nobody's getting hurt," said Bullfrog.

"How can you say that, after Kyle?"

"Listen," said Bullfrog. "I'm just trying to get us out of here while we can still fucking walk."

"Get out of the river," said Mara.

Bullfrog wiped his mouth with the back of his hand. He took another step down the stream.

"You didn't even see him at the end," said Mara, her voice rising. "You were gone. We had to do it without you."

"I was looking for help," said Bullfrog.

"I don't know," said Mara. "You seem to like being gone."

There was a crash, a flash of light; Bullfrog had thrown his bottle against a rock. He stood there breathing hard. "I was looking for help," he said again.

"Fine," said Mara. "You want to look for help? You want to walk in the river? Go walk in the fucking river. We'll be on land."

Bullfrog stared at her. Then he turned and surged forward, water splashing behind him, until he'd rounded a bend out of sight.

It was suddenly quiet. The sparkling river, the blue sky. As if Bullfrog, the mirage, had simply vanished. As if he'd never been there at all.

27

The water was cold again. Mara had forgotten it, for a while. But now her feet ached. She was afraid to look at Ashley, and then she did, and Ashley was looking back at her, standing downstream in the dappled sunlight. The water was clear, and she saw the bottom: rocks the size of fists, skulls.

Ashley waded upstream and came to Mara, and together they climbed up the bank. They sat on a damp log. It was half-rotten and gave with their weight.

"I didn't mean it," said Mara. "I didn't think he'd go."

"I know."

"It was his choice. I didn't make him, right?"

"He probably feels stupid," said Ashley. "For throwing a bottle."

"He should. He's too fucking stubborn. He needs to cool down."

Ashley didn't answer.

"We can't get hurt again," said Mara.

"I know."

"I got scared."

"I know."

"It was too slippery," said Mara. The river. Wasn't it?

She wondered if Bullfrog resented them. If he had the whole time. Without Ashley and Mara and Kyle, he could have walked and kept walking. He might have gotten out, if he hadn't kept coming back. Coming back to bring supplies, and to shoot a bear. Without him she might have died. Without them, he might have gotten to safety. Was that true? Maybe; maybe not. But did he believe it?

"He'll be back," said Ashley.

They sank onto the ground to wait. Somewhere nearby, a woodpecker drilled at a tree trunk. Drilling trees sounded like a lot of work.

After a few hours, with no sign of Bullfrog, Mara built a fire. Bullfrog had the flashlight and the iodine drops. The women had the pot. They boiled water, drank most of it, and boiled some more. Then Ashley lay down, and Mara lay behind her, fitting her body like a shell.

How strange that they had once been five. Then four, then three. Then two.

No, they were still three.

"He must be waiting for us," said Ashley. "Up ahead. He probably thought we'd follow."

"Yeah," said Mara. She felt numb. "He just needed some time, maybe. We'll sleep here and catch up in the morning."

"He'll be waiting."

"I know."

But Mara couldn't sleep. The darkness crackled and shifted

around her. As if creatures swung through the shadows, just out of sight. Waiting for her to close her eyes. She held Ashley tight, glad not to have the flashlight. It would be too tempting to use. And what would she see in the instant she flicked it on, breaking the comfort of darkness? She pictured monstrous faces, inches from her own. Eyes glowing in the trees. It was better not to know.

The fire was small, and by dawn they were both shivering. Mara warmed a pot of fir needle tea. They ate smoked bear in silence, ripping the tough meat, picking the tendons from their fuzzy teeth. There was mist on the river, and the sky was broad and white.

When they had eaten, they walked, scrambling along the bank as the sun rose high. Mara's muscles felt like loose string. Her feet swollen and raw, like they'd been soaked in acid. She took her mind from her body, removed the burden of choice, and watched her legs take one impossible step after another.

At midday they stopped to rest. It was a false rest, a rest that offered no respite, just left them to linger in the same pulsing exhaustion. Mara lay on her back, and she wasn't sure how she would roll to her side, let alone sit up again. Let alone stand.

Ashley lay on the dirt beside her. She'd pulled her hair over her face like a curtain, blocking the sun, blocking everything. Her hair was snarled in thick knots.

"If we don't find him . . ." said Mara.

"Yeah?"

But there was no end to the sentence. If they didn't find Bullfrog, they would continue on without him. It seemed horrible to say this and horrible not to.

Mara was tired of waiting for the worst, tired of pretending the worst wouldn't happen. Maybe they'd never see Bull-frog again. Maybe they'd find him in the river, facedown. His tunic rippling in the current. They would pull him ashore, and bury him, and then they would keep walking.

No, they couldn't bury him. They were too weak. They would take his belongings and cover him with leaves.

"We'll find him," said Ashley. "He knows where we are, and he won't get hurt. He knows how to walk in the woods."

"Nobody knows how to walk in the woods," Mara said. "Not like this. This isn't normal walking."

"It basically is," Ashley said. And then she said, "Mara?"

"What?"

But she didn't answer.

28

Mara," said Ashley.

"Yes?"

"Do you want to give up?"

"Do you?"

"It seems so easy to just . . . you know. Not get up again."

"Don't think about it. Just rest for now."

"What if we don't find him?" said Ashley.

"You're the one who said we would."

"But what if?"

"Then we'll keep going," said Mara. "We have food. We'll get ourselves out, you and me, and then we'll send other people to look for him."

"Mara."

"Just rest."

Mara wondered if they should go back to their old camp. Maybe they shouldn't have burned the shelter. Maybe they needed it more than Kyle did. They could have dragged his body out.

They walked again, endless. The river flattened, and the banks grew wider. The current ran south. One of Mara's sandals broke, and she carried it in her hand, limping. The forest was mostly birch now, leaves flickering in the breeze.

Eventually they came to a clear pool with a fallen log in it, and Mara could see through the water where trout hovered in the shade of the log. In another life, she would have loved to sit there on a warm evening, fishing and enjoying the solitude, watching clouds slide over the trees. Instead they sat to eat. Ashley unwrapped the bundle of smoked bear, took a piece, and handed the rest to Mara. Two of the strips were stuck together, and when Mara pulled them apart, she saw they had started to mold. She closed the bundle quickly.

The pool was as good a place as any to camp, and maybe the best they would find for the night. The moss around it was thick and cool. Mara rinsed her feet in the water, and tendrils of blood and dirt swirled through her fingers. She washed Ashley's, too, rubbing her soles and blistered toes. Ashley didn't wince. She stared blankly at the water. Then she curled in a ball, slowly, without a word.

Mara lay behind Ashley on the moss, put an arm around her. Something crawled on her leg, and she brushed it off. A few mosquitos buzzed around her face. Dusk. Somewhere people were switching on their lights. Putting leftovers back in the fridge. Lighting candles and drawing a bath.

She wished desperately that they had a bed. A king bed with white sheets and a fluffy down comforter, the kind that swallowed you, and way too many pillows, so many that they got in the way. She missed the gentle warmth of a comforter.

It was nothing like the pulsing heat of a fire or the scratchy padding of straw, and struck her now as miraculous. What did it take to make a comforter? Growing cotton for the cloth, spinning and weaving it thread by thread into a fine, fluid thing, gathering the down from geese, and all those minuscule stitches holding it together. You could go into any store and find a stack of them, packaged, ready to buy with a plastic card. As if humanity had a surplus of comforters, handing them out anywhere but here. And mattresses? Mara didn't even understand mattresses. What was foam? Leave me here for a decade, she thought, for a lifetime, and I'll never make anything half as extraordinary.

If they were in a hotel, they could sit on an extraordinary mattress, under a warm and downy comforter, and order room service, and someone would prepare a meal and bring it right to the door. Maybe even to the bed if they asked for it. They could lean on fluffy pillows and eat spaghetti with a fork and watch television that wasn't about them. Mara hoped she might dream about being in a hotel, but her dreams were empty. She woke to Ashley squeezing her arm.

"Do you hear that?" Ashley whispered.

Mara heard the usual sounds. Movement in the dark.

"There's nothing."

"No. It's big."

"Are you sure?"

"Listen."

Mara listened carefully, and this time she heard something cracking, knocking branches around. It seemed far away.

"It was farther before," said Ashley.

"It's a deer."

"Or a bear."

"Probably not. But let's build up the fire."

Mara crawled to the edge of the moss, until she felt grass under her palms, and she pulled up a few tufts by the handful. Crawled back and threw them on the fire. The grass was green, but it gave off enough light that she could find more fuel, which cast more light, until they had made the fire big.

Once it was roaring, dancing, Mara felt better. In some ways a big fire was even more comforting than a bed. They listened for the cracking sticks but couldn't hear them.

"I think it's gone," Ashley said.

"Hey!" Mara yelled.

"What are you doing?"

"It could be Bullfrog."

"At night?" said Ashley. But they yelled together, and listened.

"Did you hear that?" said Ashley.

Mara hadn't. The hairs went up on her neck. She kept listening.

It was a voice. A small voice, calling back.

They yelled back and forth as he came closer, and finally a figure stumbled into the ring of light. He fell to his knees and the women hugged him, and it was only when Mara's face felt wet that she realized she was crying. Or maybe they all were. She was almost nauseous with relief. She kept one hand on Bullfrog's shoulder, and she didn't want to let go.

She hadn't realized how much she'd resigned herself to never seeing him again. Or how much she believed that if he vanished, eventually she and Ashley would, too.

In the flickering light, Bullfrog had a black eye and lines of dried blood on his cheeks. When Ashley reached to touch them, he winced. "Just branches," he said. "It's nothing. That piece-of-shit flashlight crapped out on me."

"You came back," said Mara.

"I've been trying to get back for a while now."

"Do you resent us?" said Mara.

"The fuck is it like in your head?"

"I'm sorry," said Mara. "For what I said. I was afraid you'd die with that being, you know, the last thing you heard."

"Don't."

"And also, fuck you. We've been terrified."

"I know. I've been—"

"Don't ever pull that shit again."

"I found something," he said.

The words were so unexpected that it took Mara a moment to process. But Ashley sucked in a breath. "You found something? People?"

"Not people. I don't know what it is."

"What is it?"

"I said I don't know. I have to show you."

"So show us," said Ashley.

"In the daylight. Jesus."

Bullfrog lay down to sleep, and the sleep must have been real, the way he sank into it, a fatigue so deep that it overcame their excitement. Or maybe his was the exhaustion of relief. Mara couldn't fall back asleep. She sat up and fed the fire and boiled water until the tops of the trees turned gold. The pool was black, but eventually it turned gold, too. Ashley stirred but didn't rise. Bullfrog slept into full daylight, which was unusual. The songbirds had long quieted. Then he opened his eyes and sat up.

"Let's go," he said. "It's not far."

They walked through the morning, clambering along the bank, past a waterfall and two more pools, through a bog that reeked of sulfur and sucked at their feet.

The river grew wider, deeper. Then the landscape opened and poured into a dark lake.

Without hesitating, Bullfrog waded into the mouth of the river. He walked until the water reached his hips, splitting and closing around him. Then he looked back and held out his hand. Mara walked into the water and took it. She reached back for Ashley. With each step they fought the current. They held each other up.

The lakeshore was rocky, thick with pine. They followed it until they neared an island. "Through the trees," Bullfrog said. "What do you see?"

Mara saw trees and branches. The same as they'd seen for weeks. And then a flash, a ray of sun. But the sun was behind them.

"What is it?" she said.

"The way the light hits," said Bullfrog. "I think it's glass."

Mara turned to Ashley, to see her face. But Ashley was already in the lake.

29

Ashley swam for a long time. Her head grew smaller and smaller, a shrinking dot that flickered in the glare of the water. Then she reached the island and disappeared.

Bullfrog and Mara built a fire on shore and waited. It was a big lake and neither of them was a strong enough swimmer to follow. Ashley knew where they were. This part was hers.

"It's not that I like being gone," said Bullfrog, chucking a pebble into the lake.

"What?"

"She might just be better off without me."

"Your daughter?"

He threw a bigger rock in the lake, and it splashed. His eyes were red. So Mara threw a rock, too.

"Well," said Mara. "We like you around."

Finally there was a movement in the distance, flashes on the water, and a dark shape growing closer.

It was a dream. They were dreaming. Ashley came to them

in a canoe, and they climbed into it. It was a small canoe, riding low, and cold water splashed over the sides. There was one paddle, and they took turns with it. Whoever didn't have the paddle pushed water with their hands. For a time it felt that they were not moving at all, and then they came to the island and climbed out.

The cabin was barely visible through the trees. Without the glare of sunlight on the glass window, they would never have known it was there; it seemed a miracle that Bullfrog had spotted it at all. They pulled the canoe high on a muddy bank. Pushed through grass as tall as their thighs, and then they had reached the front step, and then they were at the door of this thing that was built and solid and real and that they themselves had not made.

The door was locked. Bullfrog felt around the doorframe and Mara turned over rocks below the window, and sure enough, under a stone, she found a key. It worked. The door opened, and they all walked inside.

It was a one-room cabin, made of logs. Maybe twenty by twenty, peaked roof with a woodstove, and a pile of chopped and ready kindling beside it. There were two cots layered with thick blankets, a wooden table, and a wooden counter along one wall. The walls were covered in shelves and hanging things, a saw and snowshoes, a fishing pole and a compound bow. All of it draped in white dust that swirled in the column of window light. Each shelf was stacked high with cans of food.

There was something strange about the place, something that made Mara uneasy, but she couldn't put her finger on it. She thought it was the shock of knowing that now they would stay alive.

Mara would have thought she was still dreaming, had fallen asleep or lost her mind, but Ashley and Bullfrog were beside her, and her subconscious could never have pictured them as vividly as they now stood. Bullfrog's chest rose and fell as his eyes darted around the room. Ashley couldn't seem to lift her feet. Mara guided her to a cot, and she sank down on it. She lifted a blanket, the ghosts of its wrinkles bleached in place by the sun.

"What is this?" said Ashley.

"Somebody's hunting camp," said Bullfrog. An odd, spreading smile on his face. He stuck his head in the woodstove and pulled it out sooty. "Chimney looks clear. They'll be back. We just gotta wait 'til fall."

The counter was lined with gallon jugs of water, warped from freezing and thawing. The survivors drank from one in turn, clear water washing their chins. They opened pop-top cans of cocktail weenies and ate them with their fingers. Droplets caught in Bullfrog's beard. Mara brought a can to Ashley and put it in her hands, and she ate, too.

Halfway through the can, Mara was filled with an incredible exhaustion, but she pushed through it to drink the brine. No sooner had she emptied the can than she lay down beside Ashley and was gone.

WHEN SHE WOKE, IT WAS DARK, THE SHAPES OF FURNITURE LIT BY FLICKERS through the glass door of the stove. Bullfrog sat at the table, staring at nothing, but he looked at Mara when she stirred.

"Sleeping beauty," he said.

He passed her a thermos and told her to drink. It was almost too heavy to lift. Hot chocolate, sweet and rich. Mara poured it down her throat, and then sleep washed over her once more, and she barely lay down before everything disappeared.

WHEN MARA WOKE, IT WAS DAY, AND SHE ATE ANOTHER CAN OF WEENIES. SHE thought she might throw up, but she didn't. She went back to sleep, where she belonged.

WHEN SHE WOKE AGAIN IT WAS DAY, AND THE STOVE HAD GONE OUT, AND EVERYONE was asleep. She rebuilt the fire and closed her eyes.

IT WENT LIKE THIS FOR SOME TIME. THE SURVIVORS SLEPT AND DRANK AND ATE. The days passed; eternity passed. Mara didn't know how many days or weeks. She didn't know how long.

GRADUALLY SHE STARTED TO EMERGE. THE CABIN WAS THE DREAM. SHE WOKE INTO it. She did not know where she was, and even when she knew, she could not make sense of it. She could hold a tin cup, with its shallow and dented bottom, could smell the wood from the stove, the chemical salt of tinned beans, the comforting stink of living bodies, the cedar of the log walls. The air was a breathing thing, and they were in it, and nothing anymore was real.

When she woke, Bullfrog was there, and when she slept he was there, too. Ashley always beside her in their shared cot, two bodies pressed close. Bullfrog was dressed like a person. He had found clothes. He wore jeans, which were several inches too short, but still they swamped his thin legs. A flannel shirt with a torn hem and big black buttons. He gave Mara a flannel shirt, too, and she didn't know what to do until he buttoned it gently up her chest and straightened the collar and cuffs.

She woke and she was Mara, in strange clothes. She slept and she was her, too.

She didn't know where she'd been. She knew about *Civilization*. She knew about Kyle. But for those first days or weeks in the cabin she was somewhere else, too, a place she could never describe. She didn't know if she'd ever go there again, or if she would recognize it if she did. She didn't know if she would choose to, given a choice.

She woke and it was raining. Pouring rain, rain like she'd never heard, pounding the tin shell of the roof like they were inside a drum. It rained and rained and everything was noise, and water crept through cracks between the logs, and still they were dry, in a cabin, in a real cabin like people should be.

Mara washed her face in cool water from a bucket. Days later, when she was stronger, she washed her hair with lake water warmed on the stove. She could not push her fingers through her hair. It was a solid object. But it dried soft, and fell into strands as it dried. She gathered the empty cans strewn around their cots and put them in a wooden box. The counter was covered with mouse droppings, and these she brushed to the floor with a wool sock she'd found between the blankets, and she had rarely seen a surface so flat or smooth.

She touched the items on the shelves, delicately, like they were artifacts in a museum. A stack of dusty books, and a notebook, which was empty. Arrows. A photo, unframed, of a woman and a boy. She opened a toolbox under the bed and found packets of seeds. She closed it tightly, slid it back into the dark.

Sometimes, Mara went outside and stood in the tall grass. Looked at the trees above her, and the emptiness of the lake. Walls of bushes, prickly, with berries just starting to blush. All those branches reaching toward the sky. Then she came in and went back to sleep.

THEY WOKE AT INTERVALS, ALL OF THEM. SHUFFLING AMONG ONE ANOTHER. BUT more often, as time passed, they were there at the same time. Awake. Sitting around the table on cut-log stools. Sitting upright was hard, and Mara grew tired from it, so they propped pillows on the cots and sat there sometimes, too.

"When does he come?" Ashley asked. She meant the hunter who built the cabin. She had washed her hair, too, and she leaned against Mara, her head soft on Mara's neck. They had both bathed from the bucket, and now they could see the colors of their own skin.

"September," said Bullfrog. "If not sooner." He had found hunting and trapping magazines under a box of headlamps, and he shuffled through them, selected one to read. He took his time before speaking. They all moved now in their own time.

"Someone'll come," he said. "Find us here. When the season opens. Gun deer season, or even bow."

That's when Mara knew what bothered her about the place.

"Nobody's coming," she said.

Bullfrog turned the page to an article about doe-in-heat urine.

"It's not a hunting cabin," said Mara.

Now it was fitting together. The layers of dust. The seeds. How the cabin was well hidden, but full of supplies. There was no road here, not even a trail. But the cabin had every-thing they needed. Everything they would need for a long time.

"It's a getaway," said Mara. "A bug out."

"What's that mean?" said Ashley.

"It means someone made this place for insurance. So he could come here and never get found." She found herself speaking quickly, saying things she hadn't known were true until she heard them aloud. "Maybe he built it for his family. His wife and his son. But he stopped coming. He never fin-ished it, or there'd be medicine, a radio . . ."

"But for us," said Ashley. "What's that mean for us?"

"It means the world didn't end," said Bullfrog, rubbing a hand through his beard. "If it did, we'd have company."

It meant that if they wanted to be rescued, they had to do it themselves.

And yet it seemed absurd to imagine leaving. Not when they had a place that fed and sheltered them, where they grew stronger rather than weaker by the day. A place that had what they needed. A place where they could live. What would they leave for? Where would they go, back into the wilderness that had killed Kyle?

And so they stayed. Bullfrog set a trapline on the main-land. He came back in the evenings with rabbits and once a spotted skunk, and he stretched the pelts on wooden frames. Mara dug an improvised outhouse in the privacy of the trees. They ate rabbit and green bean stew with salt, and pilot bread for dessert. They played cards and hangman. They found a plastic chess set, and though they only remembered half the rules, they played that, too, in the evenings, taking turns. More often than not, Mara won the chess games. "You've got the mind for it," said Bullfrog, and though she hushed him, she was pleased.

At night they went back to their old conversation, their theories about the crew. Bullfrog still swore there'd been a plane crash. Mara knew he liked it when other people brought up aliens, and sometimes she did, just so he could grumble and scoff. Ashley stayed quiet. But one day she spoke.

"I think they forgot us," Ashley said. "The crew."

"That's not possible," said Bullfrog.

"No," said Ashley. "I think it's true. I've been thinking about it a long time."

Mara was shuffling cards, and now she put them down to listen.

"Lenny's had failed projects before," Ashley said. "I think he ran out of money. They ran out of money to make the show."

"He told you that?" said Bullfrog.

"Not exactly. But he was worried about paying the crew. He kept laying people off. He left to talk to a funder. I think he didn't get the money, and he lied to the guys who were left, told them they'd be replaced, because he didn't want to tell them that the show was canceled."

"That's not the same as leaving us."

"Mistakes," said Ashley. "Overlapping mistakes. He thought the pilot would get us. The pilot thought somebody else would. Somebody's voicemail was full. Nobody missed us. They moved on to other things."

A hot, bubbling feeling welled up in Mara, startling in its intensity, and she realized it was laughter. Caught in her chest, because she was too tired to laugh. "Can you imagine," she said. "Can you imagine you're Lenny's secretary or accountant or whatever, and you're going through his records in a year, and you're like, Oh, shit, did we leave those people in the woods?"

"Yeah," said Ashley. "I mean, yeah, I think that's what happened."

"No," said Bullfrog, slowly. "No, the families would have realized. Some of 'em. They'd realize when we didn't come home. When did we leave camp, week six? Bet they sent out a search party that week. Probably found Kyle and figured we're all dead."

"Fuck," said Mara. "Fuck everything."

She felt a strange, quivering energy, like she wanted to hit something, or herself. It had been two, maybe three weeks since they'd left camp. How long did a search last, a long one? Ten days? It didn't matter. It was too late.

They could have stayed and waited. They could have left a note. But they'd hit week six, and just like that, she'd thought all hope was over. She was still thinking of it as a fucking show.

"I didn't think . . ." she said.

"People do irrational things when they panic," said Ashley softly. "Aren't you the one who said that?"

"I don't know," said Mara. Were they rational now?

"Listen," said Bullfrog, and his voice was firm. "Whatever happened, it's done. We're here now. We thought we were on our own, eh? Only difference is now we know it."

30

There were days when Ashley seemed fine. Fine enough, at least. Mara could tell right away, in the morning, when the day would be a good one. Ashley had an ease to her, light movements and light in her eyes.

When Ashley felt good, she nested. She lined up the cans on the shelves, or stacked the kindling again, or else she'd sit and watch birds through the glass window. She found chaga on an old birch tree not far away, and ground it up between rocks to make a dark tea. She'd mix in a little sugar and hand the cups to Bullfrog and Mara and sit there watching while they drank. If either of them put a cup down unfinished, Ashley stared until they picked it up again. "It's good for you," she said. "It's good for inflammation," which made Mara think of Kyle, and maybe it did for Ashley, too, because then she'd be quiet for a while.

Ashley didn't like the trapline. She felt bad for the animals. But she tended other things, washing laundry in a bucket of lake water by the stove, pausing to warm her hands. The evenings came earlier now, and they didn't like to use the lights, the batteries, more than they had to. But sometimes Ashley would light a candle and read to them from one of the books on the shelves. They were mostly trapping manuals, but she found a cowboy paperback, full of shoot-outs and lost love, and she read the dialogue in a terrible Texas accent, like she was starting once more, in her small way, to perform.

When it got too dark to read, or when their eyes were tired, they sang—old folk songs, pop songs, whatever they could recall. Mara had never been able to sing on key, but that didn't seem like a thing that mattered anymore, or even existed. Voices were just voices, except for Ashley's, which was more than that. She harmonized on the chorus. Mara built up the fire before going to sleep beside her. Days like that, it felt something like a life.

Other times were different. Ashley thrashed in the night, and Mara calmed her until her panic slowed. Or else Ashley would lie in bed late, and when Mara checked on her, she was not sleeping but staring blankly at the log wall.

Sometimes Ashley woke sobbing and didn't stop the whole day. Silent now, the way she cried. Eyes dull as tears rolled through them. When Mara touched her, she jolted. As if she'd been struck. But Mara could keep touching her, stroking her forehead, her back, until finally Ashley's muscles relaxed, and it felt like a war had been won or at least stalled. Sometimes Mara petted her for hours. She pulled the knots from Ashley's hair with her fingers, as gently as she could. There were always more knots, and they grew quickly, the way she tossed at night. Mara tried to untangle them, and Ashley let her, or maybe in times like that she just didn't care.

On those days, Mara knew better than to ask questions. Ashley wouldn't answer, and it seemed to stress her out to try. In her worst times, it was like she couldn't make sentences at all. She'd start talking and gasp, or choke on one word again and again. She worked herself into a frenzy. "I can't," she said. "I can't, I can't, I can't—"

"You can't what?" Mara asked once. Ashley opened her mouth, frozen, then began to sob so hard that it seemed like throwing up. Bones under a blanket, convulsing. She was a thousand pieces wrapped in skin. "I can't, I can't—"

Eventually Mara learned the answer.

"You don't need to," Mara said. "Don't worry. You don't need to."

AT TIMES THE WORDS ASHLEY REPEATED WERE DIFFERENT. "I CAN'T TELL YOU," SHE would say. Or, "I never." And then she'd circle back to *I can't*.

Mara remembered what Ashley had done for Kyle, telling him about himself, and she tried to do the same. Repeating details she remembered, or that she'd overheard Ashley tell the cameras. Many of them were things she didn't even remember learning. But somehow she knew.

"You're twenty-four years old," Mara said. "You grew up in California, with your mom and your sister. You're a swimmer. You like camping. Your mother's name is Doreen. Your sister is Beth."

It occurred to Mara that maybe Ashley wasn't twenty-four anymore, and she wouldn't know. Maybe Ashley didn't know, either.

"You signed up for *Civilization*," Mara said, "because you're tough and brave and you have something to show the world, and the world is going to see it. You're going to have one of those science shows. You're going to be famous someday."

When Ashley tensed, Mara knew it was time to change course.

"Or," she said. "Or you can move home and change your name and nobody will find you ever again. You can start over. You can be whoever you want."

On days like that, when Mara petted Ashley long enough that she took a deep breath, air rattling to the bottom of her lungs after hours of gasping and choking, it felt like the most important thing Mara had ever done.

31

The morning felt normal enough. Mara sat on the cot, leaning back against the wall, with Ashley curled up in her lap. Ashley seemed to be asleep, twitching and mumbling. Then her movements grew. She shook harder, almost convulsing, flailing her fists so they landed on Mara hard. Mara had never seen a body move like that, had never seen grief shake the bones. She wrapped her arms around Ashley and pinned her tight, squeezing as hard as she could. Trying to still her, to calm her, before either of them got hurt.

"Shh," said Mara. "It's okay. I'm right here."

"You don't know," said Ashley. "You don't know."

"I know it's okay," said Mara.

Ashley was still shuddering, or would have been, if Mara weren't holding her so tight. That trembling in her bones.

"I'm sorry," she whispered.

"There's nothing to be sorry about," said Mara.

"You don't know."

"Look around," said Mara. "Tell me what you see."

She would do anything, say anything, to take Ashley out of her own mind.

"We're trapped," said Ashley.

"We're not trapped," said Mara, though Ashley was, in her arms. "Tell me what you see."

When Ashley spoke next, her voice was so small, so cracked, that it seemed to come from someone tiny, someone who could fit in the palm of one hand. A ghost. A puppy who only wanted milk.

"Walls," she said.

"Tell me more."

"The window. Clouds in a blue sky."

"Good. Clouds and a blue sky. Where are you?"

"Nowhere," she said. "We're not anywhere."

"Apart from that."

"Lost."

"Yes, but apart from that. Where are you right now?"

"In the cabin with you."

Mara nodded, and the walls blurred. "Yes. That's right."

"There's flies," said Ashley, and they both laughed, and then Ashley's laugh turned back into a sob and she was shaking all over, choking like she was dying while Mara stroked her hair, choking until she could breathe again.

"It smells like smoke," Mara said. "We smell like smoke. But clean."

"Blankets."

"Flannel shirts."

"An inchworm," Ashley said, and Mara followed her gaze to the shelf. A caterpillar had reached the end of the wood and reared into space, feeling for anything, and then it bent itself in half and turned around.

"This is all that's real," Mara said. "Do you understand? This is the only thing that's real. There's nothing else. It's just us. It's just Bullfrog and us."

"Mara." In a quiet voice. "I need to tell you."

"Tell me."

They lay together for a long time. Finally Ashley spoke.

"He didn't ask me to shoot him," she said.

Mara couldn't tell if she felt surprised. She felt that nothing in the world could surprise her anymore. But she knew what she had to give Ashley, the only thing left that could help.

"He did," she said. "I heard him ask you."

"No," said Ashley. "You weren't there. It was just me, and he was moaning, and I couldn't stand it anymore—"

"I think you're so scared and sad that you can't remember. But you have to trust me. I was right there, I heard the whole thing. He asked you, Ashley. He was sure. And you helped him."

Ashley was quiet for a long time.

"I don't remember that," she said.

"You don't have to remember it. I do. I do because— because I couldn't help him, but you could. I wish you'd mentioned this weeks ago. I could have told you then. I'm so sorry you've been remembering it wrong. What a terrible thing to think."

"He asked me?"

"He was begging you, Ashley."

"Are you sure?"

"I'm sure," said Mara. "I promise."

"DO YOU WANT ME TO LET GO OF YOU?" MARA ASKED.
Ashley shook her head.

THE HOURS PASSED. BULLFROG BUSTLED AROUND, REARRANGING STACKS OF CANS.
The patches of light on the floor and the wall were fading. "Do you want me to let go of you?" Mara asked.

"Okay," said Ashley.

When Mara loosened her arms, Ashley slid to the ground like liquid. She lay there until Mara lifted her up, and brought her back to the cot, and together they lay down to sleep. Ashley slept quietly through the night.

32

A full moon came and went. The bushes were thick with blackberries that fell at a touch, thumping like raindrops. The survivors ate until their hands and faces were stained red, their wrists and fingers pricked with thorns. The season hadn't changed yet, but it would.

One morning Mara felt wet, and saw that she'd started her period for the first time since *Civilization* began. She padded her underwear with a strip of cloth. It only lasted a day, but it felt like change, like her body had decided she was okay.

They were stronger, all of them. When they first walked to the cabin, it had taken three days to cover a distance that was probably ten, twelve miles. Now Bullfrog walked half that in a morning, scouting and trapping, carrying hides and supplies. Mara knew he wasn't just out there for traps. He was searching for something, anything. An overgrown trail, an old blaze on a tree. People had been here before, and they must have come from somewhere, and left for somewhere, too. It didn't matter how long he found nothing. She knew he would keep searching. That was how Bullfrog lived, the only way he let himself live.

If they were going to leave the cabin, they should leave before the cold came, and the snow. The canoe was rickety, but maybe they could take it downstream, packed with supplies. Go on foot once it broke or the rapids grew too big. But the thought of leaving shelter again, leaving the food and the blankets and the glowing stove, was terrifying. And though they didn't say it, both Bullfrog and Mara worried about taking Ashley from the cabin. It was as if the structure itself helped to hold her fragile self together.

They could stay for the winter. Howling wind and clear white mornings, snow blown through the cracks around the door. They would stack wood by the stove, and jump in stocking feet over puddles on the floor. Choose a day for Christmas, trade handmade gifts. They'd be warm enough, and probably gain weight. Not survivors but people. Whoever made this cabin had prepared it well.

But that would mean staying seven, eight more months at least. They couldn't travel over snow, at least not together. They only had enough winter layers for one person. They'd freeze dead in a day.

"Do you think Ashley could leave?" Bullfrog asked. He and Mara had gone outside to chop wood, and to talk in private.

"She's messed up."

"Maybe *we're* messed up. Maybe she sees things clearly, and we're the ones who don't get it."

"We could stay," said Mara.

"Or we could leave."

"What do you want?"

Bullfrog split a log through the middle, one *thwack*, and it fell in two halves on the ground.

"Doesn't make much difference where you live," he said. "Winter's winter."

"But you want to leave."

He chopped another log in half.

"If we make it out . . ." Mara said, and then trailed off. That was a nice thing about Bullfrog. She didn't have to say *when*, a lie so obvious that it insulted both of them. Around Ashley, she didn't dare say *if*. "If we get out," she said, "what are you going to do?"

It was a familiar question. What they talked about, now that they didn't talk about the crew. Sometimes Bullfrog said he'd get a big steak, with curly fries and ranch dressing. Or he'd go to a resort. Take settlement money and move to the beach in Mexico. "I won't suffer another day in my life," he said. "I'll eat at different restaurants every meal. I'll order three meals at each place, and take the best bites from each one."

The way he talked, it was like he made up the answers on the spot. But he said the same things every time, so Mara knew he thought about them.

"Hedonism," she said.

"Something like that."

Sometimes his dreams were smaller. He wanted to smoke weed and watch boxing on TV. He'd buy the nicest shoes he could find, so his feet never hurt again. He'd start getting massages. Maybe he'd go to church.

But there was one dream he always came back to. He wanted to build a house for his daughter.

"I don't need to live near her," he said. Like he was reminding himself. "Fuck, maybe she still won't talk to me. But she's gotta be settling down soon. Having kids, if she hasn't—if she hasn't already. Wherever she wants to live, if she finds land, I'll build it. Five bedrooms. One of those kitchen islands, you know what I mean? Big windows on every wall."

"You can build a house for me," said Mara.

"I already did. It's her turn."

But Bullfrog seemed pleased with the comment. He chopped more wood, and Mara gathered the pieces in a pile.

"We should talk to Ashley," Mara said. "If we're gonna leave. We should just do it."

"You doing the honors?"

"I can. But not yet."

"Before the berries dry up."

"Okay," said Mara. "I'll talk to her then."

THE NEXT DAY, MARA SAT DOWN ON THE COT AND PUT HER HAND ON ASHLEY'S shoulder. "Ashley," she said. "I've been meaning to tell you something. But I haven't known how to say it."

"Just tell me."

"Well," said Mara. "This is the part where we harvest your organs."

Ashley stared at her for a long time, and then she started to laugh. She laughed and laughed.

Things were good in the cabin. They weren't perfect, but they were good. Sometimes Mara got a funny feeling in her chest, not déjà vu but close. It was the way the survivors baked corn bread in the afternoons, blending cornmeal and canned milk in a cast-iron pan, and then sat on the grass and ate it with their hands. The way the stove was always roaring when she woke. Ashley's performances, and Bullfrog's booming applause. Mara did not want to live in a city, but she understood, for the first time, why people might.

In the mornings, while Bullfrog tended his traps, Mara and Ashley sat and talked. Mara told Ashley about her parents, how they lived in a parallel world. How, growing up, she had never known if their fears were right. How she still didn't know for sure.

"It must have been lonely," said Ashley.

"I didn't think so," said Mara.

"Yeah," said Ashley. "But you got out." The irony struck them, and they both laughed again.

"It's a long con," said Mara.

"To harvest my organs."

"Surprise."

Ashley unbuttoned her shirt. "Okay."

"Funny. You're so funny."

But Ashley caught Mara's wrist in her hand, and brought the hand to her breast. Now they were both very still.

"Okay," said Ashley.

Mara didn't know what she meant.

"Touch me," said Ashley. "Whatever you want. Do anything to me. Please."

"I'm not going to do that. I'm not going to . . ." Mara stopped herself. "I'm not using you like that. I don't want to."

Though they were always together now, and often touching, they touched like puppies, not lovers. Drawn to warmth and comfort, not hunger. Not exploration. Mara had not forgotten the taste of Ashley's mouth, her skin, but it seemed like the memory belonged to someone else. Or maybe it was this distance from the past, this imaginary distance, that allowed Mara to lie beside Ashley at all without sinking back into the shame she felt about the times they had been together before. She wasn't sure what felt worse, the idea that Ashley had kissed her for television or the idea that Ashley had kissed her because she felt that she had to. Both were unthinkable. Better to pretend that the whole thing had happened to someone else. And wasn't that true? Weren't they different women now?

"I won't," Mara said again. "I'm not using you."

"You're not using me," said Ashley. "I'm using you."

"Ashley."

"Do you want to touch me?"

Mara hadn't moved her hand from Ashley's breast. Her whole body felt frozen, electric.

"Yes," said Mara.

Ashley leaned forward and kissed Mara gently, gently, on the lips. Her mouth parted, her breath shared. Then she lay back on the bed and unbuttoned the rest of her shirt.

"I don't think . . ." said Mara, and then she stopped, because she couldn't think at all.

"Good," said Ashley. "Don't think."

"You want this?"

"I do."

And so Mara touched her.

She traced her finger down Ashley's shoulder, down her collarbone and up her neck to the smooth base of her throat. The curve of her stomach, the satin skin. She raised Ashley's arms above her head and ran her hands down them, down her sides to her hips, peeled off the old jeans, every part of her raw and new from a million scrapes healing. She felt Ashley's hip bones in her hands; she massaged the length of her legs. She ran her fingers through fluffs of hair. There was nothing left on their bodies to hide. Mara traced the space between her fingers, licked her thighs and her wrists. She tasted her lips and sucked her tongue.

For a while, for a small and endless while, they found something like peace.

LATER, ASHLEY LAY IN MARA'S ARMS AND EVERY PART OF HER WAS STILL.

"Mara," she said.

"Yes?"

"The thing with Lenny—"

"It doesn't matter," said Mara. "That was a different world." Thinking of Lenny made her think of cameras. There were no cameras here now.

"I want to explain."

"I had no right to be angry. I was just scared."

"I didn't want to do it."

Mara felt cold. "He made you?"

"I don't know," said Ashley. "I just kind of went along."

"That doesn't sound like a choice."

"I could have quit the show," she said.

"Yeah, but you needed it."

"Yeah," said Ashley. She burrowed deeper into Mara's arms, and Mara hugged her close.

"He used condoms," she said.

"What a gentleman."

"Nobody said survival was comfortable."

Mara hesitated. "Maybe it should be."

"With your boyfriend," said Ashley. "Do you like it?"

"I used to," said Mara. "It's not his fault. He wants me to feel good. I just don't love him anymore."

"Do you need love? For sex?"

"Not always. But with him I did."

"And with me?"

"I don't need it," she said. "But I do."

"Do what?"

"You know."

"You love me?"

"Yes, I do." It was easy to say.

"Thank you," said Ashley, and Mara kissed her hair.

33

Two nights later, in the evening, they sat at the table and played chess by candlelight. Bullfrog played white and Ashley played black and Mara flitted between them, pointing out moves and making up rules for the parts they didn't know. Bullfrog was down to four pieces. He hesitated, then passed, and Ashley flicked over his king. He leaned back and put his feet on the table. "Your game, Mara."

She was too nervous to sit down. "I've been thinking," she said. "I think we should leave before winter."

"Leave here?" said Ashley.

"Yes."

Ashley picked up the king and set him back on his feet. "I've been thinking the same thing."

They didn't leave right away. But their days changed. No more chopping firewood or tending the traps. They went through every inch of the cabin and laid out the inventory, everything they had. For clothing: jeans and flannels, a sweater, a raincoat, one down jacket, boots that didn't fit any of them right. Bags of cornmeal, canned staples. Snares and arrows, sutures and salt. There were no backpacks. Whoever had made this place did not plan to leave.

He should have packed crates of chocolate, Mara thought. Pounds of spices. Cinnamon, turmeric, powdered cream. More books, slippers, a guitar. Toys and paints for his son. He did a lot right, but that was where he went wrong. He planned to struggle to stay alive. If Mara ever made a place like this, it would be less about struggling and more about forgetting you needed to.

She folded the blankets into lopsided packs, rolling them tight and making shoulder straps out of rope. The blankets would give them something for warmth, at least, and help them carry food along the way. Maybe ten days' worth of food, if they didn't eat much, but they were used to that by now. Who knew how long they'd have to travel? They would take the canoe as far as possible. Maybe they'd meet hunters in the woods. Maybe they'd walk for a day and find a road.

As she packed, Ashley seemed quieter. Mara thought she was just feeling thoughtful. But then she saw that Ashley's eyes were red.

"What's wrong?" said Mara. "You don't want to leave?"

It wasn't too late to stay.

"It's nothing," said Ashley.

"You can say it."

"I know it's stupid. I was just thinking about the last camp, and how we left, and now I can't stop thinking about the fish."

Mara had no idea what she was talking about.

"The fish," said Ashley. "The fish trap. We never took it apart."

"It's fine," said Mara. "I'm sure they got out."

It was a reflex, reassuring Ashley. Saying whatever she could to keep her whole.

"No," said Ashley. "Tell me the truth. Is it possible they're still in there?"

Mara had never once thought about the fish trap since they left. Now she pictured it: how carefully it was constructed, how tightly they had woven the walls. So that fish could swim in but never out. If even one fish died there, its body would turn into bait for others. The more fish came and died, the more it would become an irresistible draw.

"I think that with enough time," Mara said, "they'd be able to get out."

"You're lying."

"Yes."

"Fuck." Ashley sat down. "Fuck. What is wrong with me?"

"Nothing's wrong with you. You're trying to be kind." Mara started to say that she shouldn't worry, that cruelty to fish wasn't a real thing, but then she stopped herself. That seemed like something only fish knew.

"What if I fix it?" Mara said.

"What do you mean?"

"If I go back and take the trap apart. And then we leave."

"You would do that?"

For you, she thought. For you I would. To keep you whole. But Mara just nodded and squeezed her hand, and Ashley hugged her tight.

Now Mara had to tell Bullfrog, which seemed the harder part. He'd think the mission was foolish. Mara thought it was foolish. She found him by the canoe. He sat on a folded blanket, carving a paddle out of ash.

"Actually," he said, "I don't think it's a bad idea."

"Really?"

"I was thinking one of us should go back anyway. See what's left. Maybe there's something useful."

"That'll be weird. Seeing it."

"No weirder than anything else."

Mara had hoped that Bullfrog would talk her out of the trip.

"We're not running out of time?"

"There's always time to rescue fish."

"Shut up."

"I'm serious," he said. "No reason to leave them there, if we can help it."

"They would die anyway." Mara didn't mean it. She wanted to see what he said.

"Maybe, but not today."

Mara felt strangely happy as she walked back to the cabin. Bullfrog turned back to his wood.

It was odd to pack alone, even for a two-day trip. Some canned spaghetti, and iodine drops so she wouldn't have to boil water along the way. A headlamp and spare batteries, for the luxury of walking at night. Bullfrog gave her the spotted skunk pelt to leave behind. An offering, he said, and she knew what he meant.

Mara would wear their best boots, which were too big for her, over extra socks. A down jacket and lined jeans. The nights were getting cold now. She couldn't think yet about where she'd sleep, if she had to sleep on the way. She spent the night in Ashley's arms and rose at first light, before the sun had even struck the lake.

She paddled the canoe alone and hauled it high onto a

bank. Navigation was easy; she would simply follow the river upstream. She went barefoot in the crossing and dried her feet with grass before putting back on her socks. She had scarcely walked an hour before reaching the bog, with its sucking mud, but it was less boggy than she remembered, and she found an easy path around.

When she got hungry, she stopped and ate a can of beef soup on a low bluff overlooking the river. It seemed like the kind of place where teenagers might gather, daring one another to jump into the rapids below. Drinking and kissing as they cheered for their friends. The observation surprised her. There was no way she would have thought about teenagers the last time they passed here. She wasn't quite human then. It worried her almost, being human now, and the worry grew as she walked upstream. As if humans didn't belong here, and that was why they had to leave.

Mara passed the remains of one fire, and then another on a bed of moss. There she sat down. This was the place they had spent their first night after leaving camp. She must be close. Though there were hours left of daylight, she told herself it made sense to stop and continue on in the morning.

She could feel the proximity of their old camp. It felt like a buzzing in the air. She didn't know if the trees were different there, or the plants or what, but already the woods were familiar. She tried not to think about it. She found some hen-of-the-woods mushrooms and cut them up and cooked them in a can of pinto beans and it wasn't bad to eat. Then she put on the down coat and wrapped herself in the blanket and tried to sleep.

She couldn't. She had grown used to Ashley beside her, and now she was used to a cot. The ground was cold, and it stole the warmth through her blanket. The night was louder than she remembered, and the sounds came close. Finally she turned on the headlamp, just for comfort. The shadows were long and black, but at least she could see.

Mara couldn't tell if she wanted the morning to come or if she didn't. But like every morning, it came.

By full light she reached the far edge of their old lake and veered right, into the woods, to visit the crew camp first. The wall tents were gone, leaving patches of dead grass that were already turning back to green.

So Bullfrog was right. Someone had missed them, and come searching, and left, before they even knew it. People in this place. It made her skin crawl with longing, and something else, too—the sense that it was almost a violation. Strangers in their home. Now the strangers were gone again, and the world was theirs alone.

In another world, far away, their families were mourning. Kyle's, at least, and Ashley's. But not hers. If the news had reached them somehow, they would know she was okay.

In the bushes nearby, Mara found shreds of plastic. Raccoons had gotten into the tents, she guessed, or coyotes, and then she thought probably the bear cub, learning to live on its own, and that seemed right. After killing its mother, they'd left it a feast of bar wrappers and Mountain Dew. She hoped it had eaten well.

She lingered, gathering bits of trash until the sun was high. Then she walked the familiar path to the survivors' camp.

On the way she passed two mounds of dry scat, gray and chalky with white shards. Ash and bone. So whatever had rummaged through crew camp had rummaged through Kyle. Mara expected to feel horrified, but she didn't. She had run out of horror long ago. They had eaten enough animals here. It only made sense that animals would eat them, too.

The camp, their old home, was peaceful. That was her first thought. A simple meadow in the woods, lakeside, under a bluebird sky. Trees swaying, and a few red leaves drifting through the air. The grass had grown taller and covered the remains of their signal fires. The big maple groaned in the breeze.

In place of their shelter was a pile of charred logs. Ash had blown in all directions, darkening the grasses around it. Black lumps in a ring of soot. There was no smell.

Mara set down the skunk hide for Kyle. She closed her eyes to steady herself. And as she did, she felt self-conscious, a feeling she had almost forgotten. As if someone were gauging her reaction, judging her for it. As if she were being watched. It was the feeling of the place for her, like a stage or the set of a play. But for a moment, for the first time, it made her feel powerful.

You want me to perform? she thought to the trees. Just watch.

34

She had come for the trap.

No distance at all to the bank of the lake, the steep bank, which had felt longer and steeper when they were starving. But when Mara reached the water, the trap wasn't there. No lines of sticks tracing the surface, no labyrinth poking through. Just the smooth, untroubled water. A few red lily pads, glinting with the sun. The hum of gnats. Something splashed, modest, a turtle off a stone.

It didn't make any sense.

Mara inched closer, until the toes of her boots touched the water, and even then it was only crouching that she saw it. There beneath the glare, beneath reflected clouds. The trap was intact, but the water level had risen higher than the walls. The fish had simply swum out. She had never needed to come back at all.

Still she took off her boots and waded in. The water was colder than she remembered. The walls of the trap broke easily.

It didn't matter anymore, but she couldn't stop. Plucking one wall after another from the mud, breaking them over her flexed thigh, throwing the pieces as far as she could. Until nothing was left but sticks, scattered across the water. A few floated to the surface, but most of them sank, waterlogged, piled on one another in loose mounds that shone through the reflection of the sky. It wasn't just broken. It would never be a trap again.

Mara climbed the bank again and sat to catch her breath. The air was cold on her wet feet.

It was only then that she saw it, a glint through dry leaves. Forgotten. A camera, lying by a log, where she had once put it down and never picked it up again.

The last time they used it was the day that she and Ashley caught their first fish. A lifetime ago. She couldn't believe it was still there. As if it were waiting for her.

She picked up the camera and pressed the power button, but it didn't respond.

Batteries.

She took the batteries from her headlamp and put them in the camera. This time, when she pressed the button, the camera whirred awake in her hands.

Now Mara hesitated. She knew what she was looking for. She just wasn't sure if she was ready.

She pressed replay.

There was Ashley. Her face on the small screen, so round that Mara barely recognized it. She had forgotten that Ashley's face was once round, and even now, when she closed her eyes, she couldn't picture it that way, not until she opened them again and that full face smiled from the screen before her. Hair cascading and eyes crinkled as she pursed her lips, waiting to talk.

"What do you think?" said Ashley, posing before the camera.

And Mara's voice, from beyond the frame. "You look beautiful. Not for being out here. For anywhere."

"It's not too much?" She touched the flower by her ear.

"Not at all. You're perfect."

A hesitation. And that was when Mara saw something she had never noticed before, not when she was too nervous to look at Ashley head-on, when she could only stare down at the screen in her hands, at a sun less blinding in miniature.

In this, the video that would secure her triumph, Ashley wasn't talking to the lens. Not performing for the camera, for the endless audience. She smiled right past it. She was smiling at Mara. And Mara, looking down, hadn't seen it. She hadn't seen it at all.

"Well," said Ashley. "It's time to check the fish trap. Let's see if there's anything there. Follow me."

The camera followed; on-screen, Mara's sandaled feet followed; in Mara's mind, she followed Ashley now, too. How Ashley turned and rushed down the hill, almost skipping. Glancing back with a grin, the spark in her eyes. And when she saw the trap, she pointed, but she wasn't looking at the fish. She was looking at Mara still.

Ashley pulled off her tunic, revealing ragged skin, and walked into the water. Fitted the tunic to a ring of sticks and scooped the fish in one go. Lifted them up. Show-and-tell. That was for the audience; Mara felt the difference. And then Ashley was talking to her again.

"Mara, we did it! Oh my god. This is real. Mara. You can stop filming now. We did it!" And Mara dropped the camera to catch her, as Ashley flew into her arms. Her moment of glory on-screen, and she'd stopped the performance to be with Mara.

It wasn't a tactic. Ashley wasn't bribing her, or using her. Or if she was, it didn't matter. They were using each other. They needed each other. It was the only way to live.

Mara turned the camera off and on again. Then she turned it on herself.

Her own face looked back from the screen. Not green with darkness, but gold from the afternoon sun. Mara's hands trembled, but she wasn't hungry or cold. She had clothing now, and food. She was trapped, but she was here. She couldn't tell if she was trapped anymore. She pressed record.

"My name is Mara," she said. "I worked in Mukilteo, Washington. I came here for a television show called *Civilization*, which was produced by a man named Lenny Simmons. There were five of us in the beginning. James left. I don't know his last name. Then there were four. In early June, the crew disappeared without warning. It's almost September now. We have not all survived. I don't know if the rest of us will make it. I don't know if we'll make it out."

She told the story of what had happened. Parts of what happened. How Kyle climbed the big maple and fell while trying to signal for help. How he had asked her to amputate, but she couldn't do it. That she had failed him in that way. That he was brave and funny, even at the end. How much he loved his family. He died painlessly, she said, after holding on for a long time. He had come to peace.

She talked about Bullfrog's shelter, how it kept them safe through every night and every storm. How steady he was in his work. He was the toughest walker; he could have left them many times. But he always came back. He saved her from a bear. He found the cabin somehow, hidden in the trees, a lifeline designed to go unnoticed. And the cabin had revived them, and now they were strong enough to leave.

She talked about herself. How she had foraged, trying her best; how she had fired the flares. How, with help, she'd built a fish trap that fed them. How she had come back now to take it apart.

Ashley. There was so much Mara could say. How determined she was, and how clear-eyed. Sometimes, at the cabin, Mara felt that Ashley had broken for all of them. For her. So that Mara could care for someone, care for Ashley, and it was almost like caring for herself.

But she couldn't bring the words to her lips. She couldn't find any more words at all. She stared into the lens, searching, and then she turned the camera off and put it back on the ground.

THE SUN HUNG A FEW FISTS ABOVE THE HORIZON, BUT IT WOULD BE DARK BEFORE long. Mara had nothing more to do at camp, and no reason to spend the night. She walked a few miles and stopped at dusk by the remains of the second fire, where she ate her last can of spaghetti and slept well. When the light came, she walked on.

It was amazing the difference that boots made, that strength made. She reached the lake before her hunger had even caught up. It was a stiff paddle across the water, pushing into a headwind, but she saw a column of smoke rising and it drew her on. She opened the door and found the others, and everything was right.

Bullfrog and Ashley were playing chess and eating cold

tomato soup from an industrial-sized can. Bullfrog had his hand on a pawn.

"Game over," said Mara. "We should leave."

"Right now?" said Ashley. "I'm winning."

Mara squeezed her shoulder. "Why not? We're packed."

They had been ready for a week. Their packs lined up on the counter, as if they could get the call at any time.

It didn't take long to dress. In a way, Mara realized, they had all been waiting for someone to take the lead. Waiting for the moment when they'd know that it was right to leave. She had been waiting, too.

But there would be no signal, no undeniable sign. No promise of safety, and nobody coming to help. Each one of them was the signal. It was time to go.

They dressed simply. Flannels and jeans and boots. They had canned food and dried rabbit and dense corn bread in a cotton bag. They had headlamps for each of them, and batteries they'd save as long as they could.

"If the guy who built this ever comes here," said Bullfrog, "running from aliens or something, he's fucked."

"He won't come," said Mara. "He just wants to know he has it."

Ashley wrote a note anyway. It said *Thank you*. She nailed it to the inside of the door.

Before leaving, they had a feast. Opened the foods they hadn't tried yet. Apple pie filling, chili, refried beans and *haricot verts*. Even a whole chicken in a can, which tasted like Kyle's worms. When they had eaten all they could, they threw the empty cans in the stove. They left the fire going, locked the door, and hid the key under a rock.

They would travel for two weeks, in the boat and on foot,

sleeping curled under blankets in a row. They'd wake to the screech of a bobcat and huddle through the first snow. There'd be a waterfall, a capsize, a brief separation, and five long days of walking before they saw the lights. Before they found themselves at a ginseng farm, and knocked on the door, and a woman named Marge rushed them in, and fed them, and didn't believe their story, because what was to be believed? But she was kind and drove them to town, and there they were cleaned and admired, interrogated and clutched; and they clutched one another, too, as they found new ground, built lives separate and together. There would be lawsuits and king-sized beds and lasagna, and trips to Cancún, and meeting Kyle's sister in her cotton dress, and holding her hands while they talked. And still none of it was better than the quiet, and they found quiet, too. They found it all.

But the survivors didn't know that yet. They weren't meant to; it wasn't the way of nature. They packed the canoe and lifted their paddles. They pushed away from shore.

ACKNOWLEDGMENTS

Small Game was shaped by countless conversations. A phone call with the wonderful Esmé Weijun Wang spurred me to sit down and begin the first page. Lori Lober offered encouragement and ideas—she's a brilliant reader and a great friend. Sarah Marshall talked structure and character with me on long walks in the woods, as we watched the seasons change around us. (She is a force to be reckoned with when it comes to foraging for ramps.)

Rachael Drechsel shared her extensive knowledge of plants and mushrooms of the Northwoods. She and Colleen Michelson led me on a foraging expedition; how they can spot lion's mane mushrooms in the far distance from the back of a bouncing four-wheeler through a cloud of dust, I'll never know. Conversations with my friends Lloyd Gilbertson, Craig Fox, Owen Morgan, Jesse Krikorian, and Kathie Bollenbach helped narrow down details for accuracy.

I wrote much of the book during a winter dogsled season, living in the woods with our team of sled dogs, and I want to thank the online community around the team (hi #uglydogs!) for the friendship, laughs, and shared excitement. You all astonish me with your kindness and humor. And of course, thank you to the sled dogs themselves, who couldn't care less about a book acknowledgment but will be happy to accept pork chops of appreciation.

A few years ago I got the chance to be on an unscripted survival show, after years of being fascinated by the genre. My experience could not have been more different from the one in this book. In fact, it was the crew's and my teammates' complete professionalism and dedication, in the face of truly wild circumstances, that made me sensitive to how different the situation would be if that weren't the case: if survival was this beautiful and vulnerable with the best possible human team, what would it be like with an unscrupulous one? Thank you to Rachel Maguire, who's one of the toughest people I know, and Kip Robbins, whose presence brought warmth to all situations. I learned a tremendous amount from survivalists Gary Golding, Matt Wright, and Molly Jansen.

It was a great privilege to have Alice Truax as an early reader. She has an uncanny talent for noting exactly the things I'm stuck on, and her insight helped click key elements of the book into place.

I'm incredibly grateful to agent Andrea Blatt, whose positivity shines through everything she does. She helped *Small Game* find its place in the world and nourished it along the way. Editor Sara Birmingham has a keen eye for flow and detail, and a deep sense of story. It's an honor to be in your capable hands.

To the rest of the team at Ecco: thank you so much for the

care and passion you put into your work! It is such a delight to work with you. Thank you to TJ Calhoun, Meghan Deans, Jin Soo Chun, Miriam Parker, and Caitlin Mulrooney-Lyski.

Finally, to Quince Mountain, who's been beside me through every stage of writing (and for everything else, too). You are the love of my life and my ultimate survival partner. Every day with you is an adventure and a gift.